Charles Voysey

Theism, or, The religion of common sense

Charles Voysey

Theism, or, The religion of common sense

ISBN/EAN: 9783337263812

Printed in Europe, USA, Canada, Australia, Japan

Cover: Foto ©Andreas Hilbeck / pixelio.de

More available books at **www.hansebooks.com**

THEISM:

or,

THE RELIGION OF COMMON SENSE.

THEISM:

OR,

THE RELIGION OF COMMON SENSE.

BY

REV. CHARLES VOYSEY, B.A.,

*St. Edmund Hall, Oxford; formerly Vicar
of Healaugh.*

———◆———

1894.

LONDON:

WILLIAMS AND NORGATE,

14, HENRIETTA STREET, COVENT GARDEN, LONDON;
AND 20, SOUTH FREDERICK STREET, EDINBURGH.

Price Half-a-Crown.

LONDON:
PRINTED BY WERTHEIMER, LEA AND CO.,
CIRCUS PLACE, LONDON WALL.

DEDICATION.

I OFFER THIS BOOK, IN THE FIRST PLACE, WITH HUMILITY, RESPECT, AND CHARITY TO ALL REALLY RELIGIOUS AND DEVOUT SOULS OF EVERY CREED. IN THE NEXT PLACE, I OFFER IT TO THOSE WHO HAVE ANY MISGIVINGS THAT THEIR CREED MAY NOT BE TRUE, OR WHO MAY HAVE BEGUN TO DOUBT THE DIVINE ORIGIN AND INFALLIBILITY OF " REVELATION."

PREFACE.

THE intrinsic value of this little book will not depend on the notice that may be taken of it, or on the silent contempt that may be shown to it by the public Press. Although I am far from satisfied with it myself, and deeply bewail its shortcomings, I am nevertheless certain that, if any spoken or written words are of importance at all, what is written here is of vital importance to all truly religious souls, and through them to the world at large.

This book is a statement, more or less true and accurate, of what may thoroughly be believed and gladly embraced (concerning the sublime themes of God, and man, and destiny), without the least violence to reason, conscience, and love, which are the common properties of human nature. What is here alleged is the natural outcome of the exercise of those faculties which

God has given us for the discovery of truth concerning Himself. Of course, it is in deadly conflict with so-called " Revelation," most of all with the " Christian Revelation," although it is in harmony with much that the Bible contains, especially with the religious thought and feeling expressed by the psalmists and prophets of Israel.

The question now, not only for critics and Christian advocates, but for every one who has any sense of responsibility, is this: Which is the more true—Theism or Christianity? I do not claim for Theism that it is the *whole* truth; on the contrary, I thank God that honest and earnest men will always be discovering better and higher truths about Him and His dealings as the ages roll on. All I claim is that whereinsoever Theism conflicts with the " Christian Revelation," Theism is true and Christian Revelation is false. This is my challenge, and I demand a patient hearing and a fair encounter.

Christian advocates may be unwilling to meet me in the open field. If so, the day will surely come when their reluctance will be discovered to be due to their inability to refute my arguments and to defend themselves.

My little book contains a few simple truths upon which I have been preaching for over twenty-two years. The themes are inexhaustible and ever growing in interest, the more they are studied.

Some Theists, far more able than I am, have written on the same themes, but I stand alone in one respect. I have founded a Church and constructed a form of worship of the one living and true God, which has proved, and is still proving more and more, a spiritual help and comfort to many souls. Theism is not only a theology, but a religion. We Theists, one and all, say and feel that mere intellectual assent to the truths of Theism is of little or no value without giving our whole hearts to God in trust, love, and obedience.

We sow the seed : it may be only a grain here and there, but who can tell the mighty power of even one grain of truth ? Who can foretell what the harvest shall be ?

The following pages were written at the request of the Editor of the *Weekly Times and Echo.* I have therefore republished them as they originally appeared, thinking it would be very ungracious to conceal or to ignore help which I then regarded, and still regard, as an act of kindness and goodwill to our cause.

CHARLES VOYSEY.

St. Valery, Finchley Road,
Hampstead,
January, 1894.

The Theistic Church, Swallow Street, Piccadilly, is open for Divine Service on Sundays at 11 a.m. and 7 p.m.

CONTENTS.

———◆———

Theism; or, the Religion of Common Sense.

PART I.

Outline of Theistic Beliefs.

It is a great privilege, for which I am duly thankful, to write or speak to my fellow-men on the subject of religion. I bear in mind—and I ask my readers to bear in mind—the fact that the *Weekly Times and Echo* is read by many different sections of the community, by people in very varied conditions of life, of culture, of pre-possessions, and of natural ability for calm thinking. I must therefore write so as to be understood by all, and it may require a little patience and generosity on the part of the wiser and more advanced readers whenever I deem it needful to give explanations which they do not themselves require. It will be my object in this series of papers to state as concisely and clearly as I can what Theism is, and to lead on, step by step, so as to avoid, if possible, any subsequent explanations.

B

I.—WHAT IS RELIGION?

Very vague ideas on this subject prevail, even among educated people. Religion is frequently confounded with certain things which are only adjuncts to it, or the results of its influence. For example: Religion is not theology, nor morality, although no real religion can exist without both theology and morality. Religion is a conscious relation to God. But the very word "God" involves a theology. It will depend on our theology whether we are afraid of God, or trust and love Him. False theology teaches us a false religion. True theology teaches us to trust and love God, and so teaches a true religion.

Again, religion is not morality, but is intimately bound up with it. Morality is the chief basis on which religion is built, the root out of which it grows. Moreover, religion without morality is a sham and even a contradiction in terms. And although true religion cannot exist without bearing some fruits of morality, yet God has so constituted human nature that some people can be very moral and yet have no "religion," as above defined. (N.B.—Never be afraid of any facts, or of admitting them.)

True religion, then, is not only a state of mind in which some theological propositions are accepted as true; but it is a state of the heart, a sense of the reality and constant presence of God, a sure trust in His power, wisdom and goodness, a personal conviction of His friendliness and fatherly love, which inspires us with grateful love in return, and a strong desire to do His blessed will. This, then, is the subject before us. And it will be my duty and privilege to set before you the theology of this true religion, the grounds of reason or common sense on which it stands, and the means by which this religion may be acquired and maintained. In doing this, I shall be compelled to contrast the true theology with much false theology hitherto accepted in Christendom, and to show cause for its rejection.

Yet one word of caution. When I call Theism a "true" theology, I do *not* mean that it is absolutely and completely true; but only that it is relatively and partially true. It *is* true so far as it contradicts and annuls detected error; but it is *not the whole truth*, which will some day be gradually discovered and embraced. Even Theism, pure and high as it is above the prevailing theology, has, we are sure, some blemishes, some errors or disproportions of statement, which succeeding ages of Theists will correct; and even if Theism contained no errors at all, still the light of God's love will one day shine with so much greater radiance as to throw our present conceptions of Him into the shade. But all this frank disclaimer of infallibility and finality is consistent with the claim that our Theistic faith is unspeakably better, more true, more reasonable, more elevating and more consoling than any form of the Christian faith.

THE THEISTIC BELIEF ABOUT GOD AND HIS PURPOSES WITH MANKIND IS ONE WHICH EVERYBODY IN THE WORLD WOULD BE GLAD TO HOLD IF ONLY IT BE TRUE. It is not opposed to a single fact of science. It is not opposed to a single rational conclusion. It satisfies the keenest moral sense. It floods our life with peace, and joy, and hope, turning all our evil into good, and solving the mystery of pain and sin and death. In all this it stands out in marked superiority to Christian creeds and dogmas. Let me here state the Theistic belief in a simple common-sense way, and you can judge for yourselves whether or not my claim for its superiority be true.

We believe in only one Supreme Ruler of the world, whom we call "God our Father," whose sole purpose throughout eternity is goodness or love, goodness chosen and delighted in for its own sake and for the sake of the objects of His care. We believe that all the pains and sins and sorrows of the world are means by which God has raised and is ever raising us from a merely animal or savage state into a moral and spiritual state; that everything is working for the best, and must issue at length in the final welfare (well-being and well-doing) of every soul which He has called into existence; that we men and women *are* souls and not bodies, immortal souls and not the mere houses of clay in which we dwell; that God loves eternally *us* and not our perishing bodies, albeit He has made us capable of great enjoyment and usefulness through them. Of course we believe in a future life, and will give our

reasons for it, although we disclaim and even
denounce any attempt to speculate upon the details
of it, or on the mode of our existence after death.
It is enough for us that we shall never be separated
from God.   That changeless love of God to us, in
which we believe and rest, inspires us with love to
Him, and the desire to be as He wishes us to be;
and so hatred of sin and selfishness comes in, and
in their place we begin to love goodness, good
actions, good motives, and good thoughts, and to
love our fellow-men, and try to be to them something like what God is to us; we long to *befriend*
them.   We believe that God ordains that sin
should work misery; that it is a blessed thing for
us to be punished, especially to be tormented by
remorse and shame.   But all His punishments are
remedial, to correct and not merely to requite.
We do not ascribe to God either anger or hatred,
much less revenge.   But (to use human metaphor)
He chastises us only in love as a good father on
earth chastises his children, to amend their faults,
and not to gratify displeasure.   So, whether in this
life or the next, we cannot afford to lose any of
God's punishments for our sins, because the only
object of punishment is our own improvement of
character.

We believe in the fact of true communion with
God in prayer and praise and meditation; that it is
easier for us to speak thus in our hearts with God
than to commune with each other.   God, as Spirit,
is nearer and closer to us than we can be to our

fellow-men, with whom our bodies are the only means of communication. And we believe that it is the greatest of all privileges to commune with God directly as our Father and Friend. Mediators and intercessors are an outrage upon His love. Not only do we need none, but they are an impertinence and an insult.

And any one may say just what he pleases to God. We have no right to dictate to each other what our prayers shall or shall not be. Everyone has a child's right to go to his Father and tell Him all that is in his heart, and pour out every sorrow and every fear according to his need. But we believe God is too wise and too kind to grant any prayer that would not be a real blessing. As in a family there may be sons and daughters grown-up, and little children in the nursery, so in God's family there are souls of various degrees of development, and, therefore, some will be foolish and childish in their prayers, and others will be wise and more manly. But all may claim the Father's patient ear and loving smile and hopeful benediction ; all may give Him the earnest thanks of a grateful heart.

We believe, too, in repentance ; in true and deep sorrow before God for having done amiss. We know that God no more requires atonement or bloody sacrifices for sin than an ordinary good father on earth would. Therefore, the true condition of our regaining peace of soul and the sense of reconciliation with Him is that we are heartily sorry for our sin, and have turned our backs upon it, and will not do it again.

And we believe that as God is our Father, all men are brethren, and that the best way to please Him, and the only way by which we can possibly *serve* Him, is to love and serve our fellow-men in all the relations and conditions of life. We believe that this love of men is increased by our love of God ; and yet we cannot love God at all until we understand what love is ; and we cannot under-stand it without experience of it ; therefore we must have some love already in our hearts before we can understand that God is loving. That is why God has endowed mankind with natural human love. Hence it is that "morality" is the basis of religion. Until a man knows something, however little, of goodness and love, he can in nowise know anything of God, except His vast power and skill ; until then, he knows nothing of God to make him trust or love Him.

Of course, our Theistic faith transfigures human life with all its sorrows, sins and fears. It is a new world, all light and no darkness ; all joy and peace even amidst our tears, all hope and gladness even in the shadow of death.

Not only for you, one by one, but for all dear to you ; not only for those, but for all mankind ; not only for those whom you call saints, but no less for those whom you call sinners. One hope and glory for all. Everyone shall come home at last, the pathway being longer or shorter, easier or harder, according to the Father's divine insight into each one's deserts and needs.

For to-day I have, perhaps, said enough. If you care to know more about Theism, I will tell you next time on what our faith rests. Meantime, I will encourage your curiosity by telling you that our faith is built on facts, and not on any so-called revelation or mythological gospels.

PART II.

(*a.*) *Why " Revelation" is not to be Trusted.*

(*b.*) *Proofs of the Existence of God.*

I HAVE already stated the Theistic Faith as a heartfelt conviction of the perfect love, friendliness, and trustworthiness of God; and that what He is to one, He is, and will be, to all mankind. My present duty is to give proof of the assertion—to state the facts on which it is based. But our first step must be to explain our rejection of so-called " Revelation." Most Christian people only believe in a God at all on the ground that the Bible is His written and inspired and infallible Word or Revelation to men. A large number of Christians put the " Church " in place of the Bible, and claim that it is a Divine institution, likewise infallible, to teach men what is true concerning God, and to guide them in all matters of duty. Take away the Bible, and many would become Atheists, and, perhaps, worse. Take away the Church from the other party, and they, too, would drift into Atheism and immorality. Neither party have any ground, so far as they can see, for believing in God or trying to be good, beyond the alleged Divine authority of the Bible and the Church. Now it has come to pass in this age that some men, believing in and loving God much more than the rest, have discovered serious errors in the Bible and in the dogmas of the Church. These errors are not merely literary, historical, scientific, but moral and religious. In many places in both Testaments, and even in some words ascribed to Jesus Christ and his Apostles, the teaching concerning God and His dealings with men is deeply false, because it is immoral. It attributes wickedness to God, fills the mind with abject slavish fears, drives out all trust and love towards Him, killing true religion, and turning hope into despair. And when it tries to assuage the terror created by its impious threats, it only does so by blackening still further the face of our Father in Heaven, and by drawing our hearts' affections away from Him, to fix them upon a Saviour more merciful and humane. All this is true, especially of the New Testament, and the Church's dogmas.

Finding these moral blemishes in these alleged "Divine revelations," we are forced by our reason, conscience, and natural affection to say that they are not true, that God had no part nor lot in their production, and that they originated solely in the darkness, ignorance and vice of the lower part of human nature in days long gone by. Men had been not only making God in their own likeness, which was inevitable, but the lower conceptions were clung to long after they ought to have been outgrown; and worse still, being regarded not as human, but as Divine, they were placed beyond reach of amendment or rejection. People were afraid of disputing their Divine origin under the threats and curses invented to maintain a belief in them. It is so to this day. If the superstitions and falsehoods of the Creeds and Gospels were propounded to-day for the first time, they would be met with a howl of mocking incredulity. No sane person would listen to them. But they are held in a trembling reverence now, only because the mass of Christians have never dared to question the Divinity of the authority in whose name they have hitherto claimed acceptance.

But when I read that "without doubt I shall perish everlastingly" if I do not think rightly of the Trinity, I laugh that threat to scorn. Even though it be the voice of a Church hoary with the centuries, it is to me only the croaking of human ambition to crush me under its heel. And when I read that "many shall seek to enter in (i.e., to be saved) and shall not be able," I know full well that I am listening to a poor deluded fellow-man, and not to the living God incarnate on earth.

So the Theist cannot go to the Bible, or to the Church, or to the words of Christ in the Gospels, to learn submissively, and without question or criticism, the truth about God and human destiny. We still love and prize a great deal that is in the Bible, and even some words of the Church's teaching ; but it is only because we find those words to be true, in contrast with much more that is false. We cannot make an authority of that which we criticise. The moment we begin to say this or that is wrong, is mistranslated or misinterpreted, we disclose the fact that we think we know beforehand what God *ought* to have said. We thereby place ourselves above the Revelation, and it ceases to be our infallible guide and authority.

Now all this preliminary attack upon "Revelation" was necessary before showing you the grounds on which our Theistic Faith rests. Some of your clergy or ministers will tell you that because our Theism is to be found in the Bible— *e.g.*, in parts of the Old Testament especially— therefore we learnt it from the Bible, and we are dependent, like them, on Revelation. Our full answer to this will be manifest as we proceed ; but for the present it will suffice to say that we never had even a suspicion that pure Theism was to be found in the Bible until long after our faith had been built up on grounds of natural reason, or, as I prefer to call it, common sense.

I hope I may have among my readers some of those very rare persons who do not believe in a God at all. Such as these may justly refuse me a hearing altogether, if I set myself to write upon what they would call an unproved and unprovable assumption. I have observed that, for the most part, men are Atheists only in rejecting those crude and more or less immoral pictures of God with which they have been familiar since childhood. I mean that they, perhaps, would not be Atheists towards a conception of God which does no violence to reason, offers no contradiction to science, and harmonises with their moral instincts. I do not know whether I can be of any service to them, but at least I am bound to try. Let the accustomed name of God be set aside for the present. Let us begin at ourselves. Let us hold fast to facts. It is an undisputed fact that we are intelligent beings. By reason of that intelligence in us, we discern the working of intelligence in the world around us, and in the construction of our own complex nature. That is to say, the cosmos is what it is, not by chance, but by set purpose. It is crammed full of actions which (judging by ourselves as intelligent beings) can only be due to one or more intelligent wills; manifesting, it is true, far more skill and power than we possess, but acting of set purpose to achieve a result more or less remote. We cannot face a tree or a cow, much less a sun or a planet, without being at once convinced of the existence of an intelligent will, which, in whatever way, or by however long a process it has worked, was working and is working to a given end. Next, we notice that all our true science is but the discovery by us of knowledge already possessed in its completeness by the mind which planned it all. Every discovery, every generalisation we make is part of the grammar of the language of

Nature which we are learning. The laws which we are only by slow degrees discerning were there and in action before we began to think and to pry into them. They will go on acting after we are gone. But, because they are laws, they imply and involve intelligence, for we find them more and more interdependent the longer we observe and the greater our light. Thus science gives every encouragement to believe the cosmos to be the product of only one and the same mind, and gives no encouragement to, or belief in, two or more Gods, and has no place at all for a Devil.

Now, this active mind in the cosmos is, to a certain degree, cognate with mind in man. It is the same faculty in both, or else God does not know the multiplication table or a single proposition in Euclid. If He does know this, He and we, so far, stand on the same ground and have a kindred nature. I am well aware, and I have no fear in facing the fact, that the Author or Ruler of the world is by us incomprehensible. The mode in which an omnipresent power and knowledge can exist is for us hopelessly inscrutable. But all our profound ignorance of that and other mysteries does not prevent our using our common sense, and so attaining quite sufficient knowledge and assurance of the existence and knowledge of the Supreme Being. We do know that He is, and that He knows. The word " know " may be captiously objected to, because *we* gain knowledge by ways and means, while His knowledge is not acquired, but absolute and eternal. But for all practical purposes the word "know" answers well enough. If I see a horse in the street, I know it is a horse. Common sense tells me that God knows it is a horse, too. The fact that it is a horse must be as well known to Him as to me. The knowledge of the fact, small as it is, is sufficient to prove to me that my mind bears some likeness to His mind.

From Him you cannot escape. You cannot, even if you try, shut out the idea of such a God from your thoughts. Every object you see, and every reflection of your own mind, forces you to believe in His existence as a matter of fact. No assumption at all; but as much a proof to you of His being as is your own eyesight a proof that there is light.

The good people, for whom I am chiefly engaged in these papers, must kindly forgive this more private discussion with the unbeliever. Moreover, it is needful for them to see that even our faith in God's existence at all rests on plain facts—facts obvious to common sense. These grounds of pure reason are immeasurably more sure than the rotten props of "Revelation."

Having proved the existence of an intelligent God, our next task will be to prove that He is what we believe Him to be—the loving Father and Friend of all mankind.

PART III.

Proofs of the Goodness and Love of God.

POWER and skill, however vast, do not necessarily inspire the human soul with feelings of reverence and adoration. If all we know of God was that He was possessed of unlimited power and matchless ingenuity, we should not of necessity love and worship him, for He might be malignant towards us, or altogether indifferent to our moral welfare. So my readers would do well if they pressed me for the proof, which I have promised, that God is one whom we may trust and love.

Bibles and churches give no proof except in a very roundabout way. At best, they come to us at second-hand. They are not God's thoughts, but only records of men's thoughts about God—sometimes good and lofty, at other times bad and degrading. Accepted as final authorities, they represent God now as holy and loving, now as unholy and vindictive ; now as man's friend, now as man's foe. Instead of such testimony as that, we want proof that God is entirely good and trust-worthy ; that His purposes are absolutely and universally loving unto men.

The principle laid down by Theism—by common sense in thinking about God—is that the mind, or disposition, or moral character of God can only be inferred from His works and products, and inasmuch as man, in his highest aspect as a moral and spiritual being, is the noblest work of God of which we know anything by actual experience, our search for the moral attributes of God must be prosecuted chiefly in examining the higher part of man's nature. And we must bear in mind at every step of our enquiry this Theistic axiom : *God must be at least as good Himself as the best of His creatures.* He may be ever so much higher and better, but He cannot be below them. This axiom is a two-edged sword. It not only enables us to attain the loftiest conception of God possible in any given age, but it enables us to cut down to the very roots every allegation of " revealed " religion which is untrue. Every text, every dogma, which paints God as morally inferior to the best human character, or to the best human conception of God, is at once seen to be false.

The first fact which I bring forward in proof that God is good—*i.e.*, just, righteous, pure, truthful, faithful, and generous—is that we are moral beings, that we have a moral sense or " Conscience " as we call it, which urges us always to do what we believe to be right, and to refrain from doing what we believe to be wrong. Moreover, this conscience urges us to take utmost pains to find out which is right and which is wrong in any given alternatives of conduct.

Further still, the conscience in man scrutinises the *motives* as well as the behaviour, and even more than the behaviour. Conscience demands from us that we should do right without any desire for reward, and should refrain from wrong-doing without any desire to escape punishment. Our conscience does not approve us whenever we act only from "self-interest," no matter how right our conduct has been. Neither does our conscience blame us if we have done wrong through sheer ignorance, while thinking we were doing right. So this moral sense, which is the common property of mankind, reveals the purpose of God in having made it part of our higher nature. It is designed to make us good ; not merely to regulate conduct, but to purify and elevate character, to refine our most secret springs of action, and to enable us to become good at heart, good from deliberate choice and preference for goodness.

Still further, we are taught by the conscience to see that the true welfare of the world at large is only to be secured by each man doing his duty to his brother-man. So that, while the proximate purpose of the conscience is to make each man good, the ultimate purpose is to make the whole world happy. (Of course, I take happiness in its highest Theistic sense here.)

Now go back with me to our starting-point.
God is to be morally measured by His works—the
best of His works. The conscience in man is one
of the best of His works, having only good for its
object, and universal good into the bargain ; and if
God cannot be below the best of His works, He is,
at least, equal to man as a moral being. God, then,
is Himself intrinsically good—good from free choice
of goodness, good in His purposes—never, in any
form or degree, evil. He is thus proved to be a
trustworthy God, a most friendly God, a God who
is intent on the highest welfare of the creatures
under His control, and therefore He is a God to be
thoroughly trusted everywhere and always. Just
as the wonders of the cosmos prove the existence of
a mighty and wise God, so do the wonders of the
moral sense within us prove that that God is
righteous, and faithful, and true. And the charm
of this proof is not only its simplicity, which everyone can understand, but also its universality, which
every sane moral being can verify for himself by a
little calm thinking. It is *not* second-hand. It is
your and my reading at first hand God's own words
written in our consciences. Everyone carries *that*
Bible in his own breast until by persistent violation
of his conscience he strikes it dumb. After a little
space I shall deal with the objections, more or less
captious, which have been brought against this
proof of the Divine Goodness. But all I desire now
is to drive it home and make my readers *feel* that it
stands to reason that if God be the Author of the

conscience in man, He Himself must be good, and at least as good as the best moral being whom He has made. Everyone knows, without being told, that his conscience somehow reminds him of obligations to God; that he cannot sin against his fellow-man without a sense of having sinned against God too, and at the same time, and by the self-same sinful deed. And everyone knows that it would be absurd to feel this sense of sin towards God, if He were an evil God and delighted not in goodness, but in evil. The *facts* of our own experience thus corroborate the facts made known to us by observation of other men. The goodness of God is no longer a pious assumption but a demonstrated fact.

Yet, above and beyond even the conscience, we are endowed with a gift still more precious and exalted. It is "the unspeakable gift" of LOVE. This most sacred of all human words has, I know, been applied to feelings in us which are the very opposite of love, to the most base and brutal selfishness, to unlawful and degrading appetite, and is, perhaps, more than ever a misnomer when we talk about "self-love." But I appeal with confidence to the ordinary mass of men and women, and ask them to say if they do not know perfectly well what true love is. There is love in the world as pure, as perfect, as unselfish as it can possibly be. The love of a mother for her babe, and of the true father for his children, are standing types of the purest and most unselfish love. We know it at once, whenever we see it or feel it, by the conquest it makes over our lower nature, by the sacrifices so gladly, so rapturously, offered for love's sake. True love is intense desire to do good, and the highest good, to a fellow-creature, and that at all cost to oneself. In fact, the more we sacrifice for it, the better we are pleased. Nothing counts beside it. Everything else is dross.

To analyse love and to talk plain prose about it seems almost a profanation ; yet, because we are thinking now, and not giving way to mere senti-ment, we must put our thoughts into dry and formal words. If you try to think what love does and is intended to do, as the chief factor in human nature, it will tell you more about God than anything else can.

In the first place, love makes every duty a pleasure. It turns all drudgery into a delight. If we love any one truly we shall do our duty to him not for mere conscience' sake, not driven to it by a sense of obligation which we should be glad to be free from ; but we shall do our duty with a willing and glad heart, delighted to do it, delighted that it costs us something to do it well.

Illustration would be endless, but everyone knows that love is the strongest impulse for good that was ever heard of, that it breaks down every barrier of human sin and selfishness, and makes the path of duty and virtue to be rich in pleasantness and peace. If all the world obeyed their consciences, there would be no offence one against another ; but the stern justice which would prevail, and the exact performance of every obligation might be over-clouded with melancholy and secret discontent with the burdens we were called upon to bear. We might all do our duty, but have a canker, at the heart, of sadness, because we could not have our own way and do as we listed. Surely it would be a dull and severe world; and men only governed by a sense of duty could not be very happy—if that were all. So God, in His forethought and bounty, has given us, beside the conscience, the power to love those to whom we owe duties, so that the fulfilment of them should be our exceeding great reward, that we should find our highest pleasure in serving and succouring our fellow-men. Most of us know what we ought to do well enough. The trouble with us is how to get ourselves to do it. We want the impelling force. Threats and bribes have been tried long and in vain. They are power-less when compared to the impelling force of love; for love is not a *driving* power at all, but a *winning* one. It draws and does not drive. It is the spontaneous leaping up with joy to do the task which we have been dreading or trying to evade. This is seen in God setting us duties to discharge, and making it a delight to fulfil them; giving us the sweet impulse from within to do them freely of our own will and choice, and with a rapture that turns sacrifice into ecstasy. And now we behold in God a Being who understands and knows what love is, and who has given to us all a little share of it, that the fulfilment of His laws may be the means of our enjoying the highest happiness obtainable. And love is, in some measure and form of it, to be found everywhere. It comes to greet every new-born babe ; it provides for the weak, the defenceless, the oppressed ; it is the frequent healer of disease and the consoler of sorrow ; in its bosom lie wrapped all the loveliest virtues which have adorned humanity ; it enforces truthfulness, it inspires courage, it gives fortitude ; its patience is never wearied, its mercy and forgiveness are boundless. Out of human love, especially as it is seen in domestic and family relations, come nine-tenths of all the goodness which men attain, and of all the good deeds of their lives. Love is the means by which we raise and refine others while we are raising and refining ourselves.

On such a theme one never knows how to stop. I must break off abruptly, and recapitulate what has been said :—

1. God knows and has intelligent purposes. This is proved by our possession of the faculty of reason.

2. God is good and trustworthy. This is proved by the facts of our moral nature, by conscience and the high place in which we cannot help regarding it.

3. God is loving and infinitely worthy of our gratitude and love. This is proved by our own human love, and by its results when manifested in its highest form. Any truly good and kind-hearted man would, if he could, make every

other life at least end in perfect goodness and happiness. If he only had the knowledge how to do it, and the power to do it, he would do it. Therefore God will do it, because He has the requisite power and knowledge, and has a loving will not less loving than our own.

These are *proofs*, and not mere guesses. The indisputable facts of our nature are the grounds on which rest the perfect Friendliness and Fatherly Love of God for us all.

PART IV.

———•———

Influence of Theism on the Life.

I have proved already, on grounds of pure reason, the existence of a Supreme Being of matchless power, wisdom and goodness, who loves us with a changeless love, who is the Father of our souls and our best Friend.

It is obvious that if this be accepted as true, so far as it goes, it ought to have an enormous influence on our hearts and lives and character. A mere cold intellectual assent to it, simply because it is irrefutable, will have little or no practical effect.

Suppose one of us to be in some great difficulty from which he cannot extricate himself, or under some terrible fear which he cannot shake off, and then he were to be told of a kind and able friend who could and gladly would release him from his fear and overcome all his difficulties. The sufferer might believe this in a sort of way, might not find any cogent excuse for not believing it, and yet he might forbear to seek the help of that unknown friend. He might assent to the assertion of this willingness and power to help him, but still lack sufficient conviction to avail himself of it. It is precisely the same in regard to Theism. Its propositions may seem reasonable and true ; those who listen to them may be willing to assent to them ; but unless they are convinced, unless they feel the truth of the assertions, they will remain unmoved and unaltered by them. Once firmly convinced, once feeling deeply the necessity for themselves and for all mankind of such a God of goodness and love, the belief in Him is no longer a mere theory or set of reasonable propositions, but becomes an intense influence on their hearts and lives, affecting all they do, and think, and say.

The great question, " Is life worth living ? " to which so many vain and mournful answers have been given, is one that can only be answered when the true purpose of life is seen ; when the origin and cause of life are properly apprehended. Human life is most certainly part of a plan, and not the result of chance or chaos. It is in our power to discern something, at least, of its purpose ; and as soon as we learn what Theism teaches about God, we perceive likewise that God has caused us to see that He is the fountain-source whence we derive all the faculties of our higher nature, and the existence and duration of our bodies. We see, then, that our life here on earth is mainly designed to lift us as moral, spiritual beings above the merely animal and material, to raise our character, to elevate our aspirations, and to make progress possible in all that is worth knowing, and doing, and being. So far, this concerns the individual; but we are placed in groups, in families, districts, nations, races, with the purpose of helping and benefiting one another. The purpose of everyone's life is to serve and befriend his fellow-man. His opportunities for doing this are countless and incessant. All his nobler faculties are given to him for this end; his reason, conscience, and love are unaccountable if severed from this primary function of doing good and being a blessing to others. And in this is revealed to us the love of God in having given us life, the double life of the soul and the body, the life of the body as an adjunct and agent to the life of the soul. The soul exists for its own sake; for God's sake, because He loves it; and most of all for the sake of mankind, for whose well-being it is to live and grow perfect. We, then, are souls, and not bodies. The body is a sacred thing, to be cherished by us and reverenced; never to be profaned by neglect or misuse, never to be befouled by excess or unlawful appetite, but always to be used under the ceaseless control of reason, conscience, and love, for the welfare of man and the honour of God. Still, the body is only a tool, an exquisite and wonderful machine, put into our hands for a time— God's time—to use rightly, but not to keep for ever; but when it has served its turn it is to be laid aside and parted from in calmness, and trust, and hope. It was never meant to be more than a temporary lodging for the immortal soul ; never meant to be anything but the willing and able servant of the God-begotten soul within.

If once we see the distinction between the soul and the body—between ourselves and the houses we live in—the whole aspect of that vast question " Is life worth living ? " becomes changed. So long as the word " life " stands for the life of our mortal bodies alone, the problem is insoluble. But if by " life " we mean the life of the soul, then we see the infinite value of living. We answer the question with our most emphatic " Yes," and begin to view the life of the body in an entirely new light. The proportions are altered. Heretofore we put the body first and the soul second, or forgot it altogether. Now we put the soul first, and the body as subordinate. And all this reflection is needful to our right understanding of the enormous value of believing in a God who is our Father and Friend. If we were bodies only, if we were only animals, we should not need to recognise or to believe in any God at all. We then should have nothing better to do than to rake together all the "good things" of this world within our reach, to make our bodies as comfortable as we can, to gratify every appetite, and to defend ourselves from annoyance, loss, and disappointment. The world would then be a great pig-stye, only ten thousand times more foul and horrible than anything yet heard of in human or animal history ; *but no one would be aware that there was anything wrong in it.* But if we are souls, and if we know it, we shall not be able to do without religion, *i.e.,* without a clear consciousness of God and a deep conviction of His righteous rule over us and His loving purposes with us. For the reason, conscience, and love in man speak to him loudly and incessantly of his utter dependence on the Author and Giver of life. Man sees the action of an irresistible Will in forces which create, preserve and destroy, without any deference or reference to human hopes or fears. Trouble and anguish fall alike on the innocent and on the guilty ; the forces in Nature do not discriminate, by any moral test, between the victims they crush and the lucky ones who escape. The body is the sport of her wildest freaks by catastrophe, by disease, and by torture. No sane person would deliberately insist on the certainty of life, though many happily forget its uncertainties. By reason, then, man is forced to acknowledge his abject dependence on a Power outside himself for mere bodily life.

Yet the conscience teaches a deeper sense of dependence still. Under its influence, we feel beholden to a Moral Ruler whose rights over us we cannot ignore. " Conscience doth make cowards of us all," and though the terror which it begets is wholesome and good—better far than to be indifferent or presumptuous—that fear of punishment belongs not to the nobler part of man's nature, but to his lower; it is bodily, not spiritual; it is craven, not man-like; it would mislead, if not soon made away with for a sentiment more noble. Our sense of dependence grows into a sense of obligation, and this reacts upon the soul, making it cry out more than ever for the Living God. The sin which made one at first run away and hide from that Presence, now, in our better state, makes us draw nigh and plead for help and blessing, plead even for correction and judgment rather than be left unaided in the great moral struggle, or be left uncleansed with a lingering longing to sin again.

When once we have our eyes open, and stand face to face with the duties we owe to our fellow-men (not to speak of any duties we owe to God Himself); when once we have full consciousness how weak and frail and selfish we are; when once we see that all progress in virtue, all real growth in nobility of character, all elevation of our motives can only be accomplished through severe and strenuous conflict with our lower nature;—*then* we feel the full need of God; then we feel how dependent we are on a strength higher than our own; then we are drawn to that unfailing, faithful Friend as our only Refuge from our weak and wavering selfish selves.

Yet nothing makes us feel so dependent as our natural human love. Many a man is brave and heroic, facing danger for himself with no trembling step or quivering hand; grand and fearless, and almost divine, in his scorn of personal injury or death, as he rescues some poor forlorn stranger in mortal peril. But the same brave man will tremble as a child, and quiver like an aspen leaf in the presence of a danger to any one whom he loves, when it is a danger which he cannot avert. Aye, the soldier, facing without flinching the hideous carnage of the battle-field, trembled and wept, wept and trembled, when he bade farewell to his wife and child. He could not help his fear, when he bethought him of all the dire chances which lay between him and ever seeing them again. And the anxious father and mother, bidding good-bye to a son not over-fortified against the wiles of the world and the frailties of youth, must need feel their hopeless, helpless incapacity to guard him from evil.

Every day and all day the loving heart is torn and tortured in anxious fear for others, and would be soon demented altogether, but for the Refuge to which it flies. To Him it springs upward and lays the burden at His feet. It says " Lord, Thou knowest!" It may or may not beg for the protection it craves; but it is enough to behold the loving Father's face, to remember that not even the sparrow can fall without His will; and then the heart, however sore, in *that* Presence has no more fear. If the worst should befall, it will not be evil, but only good; an unspeakable blessing hidden from eyes which could not see it; a blessing believed in and hoped for by a heart which trusts the goodness and love of the Eternal, Righteous Father.

Not in a spirit of enforced and slavish submission; still less in a spirit of blind fatalism; but with clear vision that Eternal Love can do no wrong, it cries out of the depths of a satisfied conviction, "Father, not my will, but Thine be done!"

God alone can measure the sense of dependence created by the reason, conscience and affections of man.

PART V.

———•———

On Prayer.

WE have traversed the ground of facts on which our belief in a righteous, loving God is based, and we have seen how necessary it is that we should not only have a right intellectual conception of God, but also a deep and heartfelt conviction of His universal goodness and love, which shall influence our conduct and character. Our next step must be to speak of the first instinctive action of a soul thus impressed. This is the act of prayer.

"Prayer" is a word so variously understood and applied that it will be necessary to clear our minds from all confusion of thought respecting it before we can see whether it be reasonable or not to pray.

The most common meaning of prayer is petition, asking earnestly for something. Such prayer is continually being offered by man to man, and is so natural in case of need that it requires no explanation. We all know perfectly well by our experience, from childhood upwards, how to pray.

D

Prayer is a term often applied to the use of set forms, in set times and places, addressed to God, or to mediators, saints, and angels. But this is not true prayer unless the heart's desire goes up with the spoken words. The saying of prayers is not necessarily prayer.

Prayer, moreover, is considered by some to be a power possessed by man to move or alter the will of God. We are falsely taught in words ascribed to Jesus Christ: " Whatsoever ye shall ask in prayer, believing, ye shall receive." " Whatsoever ye shall ask the Father in my name, He will give it you." This we not only know to be untrue, but we reverently thank God that it is false. For if it were true, it would have the effect of transferring the government of the world from God's hands into the hands of ignorant and foolish men.

Another and more true aspect of prayer is that it is the natural communion of the human soul with the living God. It may or may not include petition, but it is, first and foremost, the real movement of the soul towards God ; the conscious turning of our thought to Him, and the silent or spoken out-pouring of our feelings and wishes before Him, as when we commune with any one we dearly love on earth. The questions which would be put by an accurate and reasonable man in regard to such prayer would be probably these :—

1. Does God Himself wish for our prayers ?

2. What benefit can we rightly expect from them ?

In answer to the first question, we say that if God be such as we have already described Him to be—knowing all things, bent only on goodness, and filled with love towards us ; even if He be only equal in goodness and love to a good earthly father—then it is inevitable that He should desire His children to come to Him, to speak to Him, to confide in Him all their wants and sorrows, and to ask for His guidance in their perplexities, and for His help in doing what is right.

If the love of God towards us be more, and not less, than an earthly parent's love, then God must desire us to pray to Him. But there is a stronger proof of it than this reasoning affords to be found in the fact that so soon as we really believe in such a God, our hearts cannot help going to Him in prayer. We are so constituted, it is such a positive law of our being, that prayer is an immediate consequence of the conviction that God is our loving Father and Friend. It is, in fact, He who thus draws us to Himself; it is the spirit of the Father in the spirit of the child, which makes the mutual attraction inevitable.

It is hardly possible in human nature for any one to know and trust in an earthly friend and yet not to seek any converse or communion with him. The law of our being makes such communion inevitable. The loving intercourse between parents and children is a perpetual witness to this fact of our nature. Therefore we may be sure that the Father of our souls loves to see His children drawing nigh unto

Him in prayer, seeking the comfort and help of His presence: "When Thou saidst, Seek ye My face, my heart said unto Thee, Thy face, Lord, will I seek."

2. What benefits may we rightly expect from prayer?

Of course all depends on our having a right idea of prayer. We cannot expect to turn God from any one of His purposes. If we could, it would be our bane and not our benefit. We cannot expect to work any miracles, to subvert or to supplement the course of Nature; if we could do so, our very prayer would be an impious sin. The true and the highest idea of prayer is communion with God, as a child with its father; but with absolute trust in His greater wisdom and love, and therefore correcting all its native hopes and desires by the wish at the bottom of the heart: "Not my will, but Thine, be done."

Yet, inasmuch as all souls have not yet attained to this manly standard, as many are still childish and ignorant of what is best for them, they still pray for things, still go on begging God to let them have what they want, and to have their own way. It is just the same in a human family. There are the infants, the young children, the boys and girls, and the grown-up sons and daughters; just in proportion to their ages and mental development, their prayers to their parents vary in wisdom and good sense. The little ones ask for impossible or injurious things; the elder, more wise, ask only for

things profitable, or, more likely still, cease to ask
for anything at all, unless it be good advice or help
in some difficulty. Shall we condemn all people
for praying who do not pray wisely and in a manly
spirit? Is prayer of no benefit when associated
with ignorance and childishness? I do not think
so. I think that every one, according to his
spiritual age or stature, according to his immature
or matured development, has a right to pray as he
pleases, to pour out before his loving Father whatever be in his heart, to ask even for impossible or
injurious things—for those very things which he
will one day thank God for refusing to grant. I say
we all have a Divine right to tell to God our most
secret hopes and desires, and to use a child's
privilege of carrying its care to a loving Father's
ear.

And I go on to affirm that even in such childish
praying there is enormous benefit to the soul. The
practice intensifies and strengthens the tie between
the soul and God. Sooner or later all the childishness will be outgrown and all the benefit of daily
communion with God will remain. For the essence
of all prayer is the recognition of the fact, and the
realisation of the fact, that God is our true Father
and we are His own children, we the objects of His
ceaseless love, He the loving Friend in whom we put
our ceaseless trust.

That Father and Friend is the greatest and most
important fact in the universe; and to live without
remembering and acting upon it is the greatest folly.

But if it be a benefit even to offer childish prayers, how much greater is the benefit of a more enlightened and manly communion with God!

As we grow older and wiser, we cease to besiege God with petitions for physical and temporal good, and we begin to care far more for moral and spiritual advancement. It is only when we put away childish things that we see the unspeakable superiority of the interests of the soul over those of the body; and nothing assuredly was ever heard of which keeps up that vivid perception so much as constant prayer and communion with our Father. The benefit of it is essentially moral. It intensifies conscientiousness, it reminds us of our obligations to God and to each other; it deepens within us the sense of shame when we have done wrong, and when we have neglected some duty; it makes us scrutinise our motives, remembering that God knows the inmost secrets of our hearts, knows our own tendency to deceive and excuse ourselves. We not only confess before Him in true sorrow our misdeeds, but beseech Him to cleanse us from our secret faults, from the defects and impurities which, in our blind self-conceit, we do not always see.

Prayer is thus the safeguard and the very life of character. It is the best known means of making us better from day to day. And I appeal, without any fear of contradiction, to my fellow-men, one and all, to say if it be not true that the men and women who truly and habitually pray to God to help them to be good are the most trustworthy of all persons. Even the wicked and the irreligious will choose the best characters they can find to become the guardians of their children and property, and to put in a position of trusteeship, wherever honesty and sterling integrity are required.

The benefit which every praying soul derives is not confined to himself, but spreads welfare and blessing on all others with whom he has to do. He who makes a friend of God becomes more and more a true friend to man. So even on the low ground of utility it is good to pray ; good for the individual, and good for mankind at large.

And they who pray can testify to the comfort and hope and joy which constant communion with God always brings. The lamentations which fill the air would be turned into songs of praise, if only the sufferers and the mourners knew, and acted as if they knew, what a friend they have in God—able, willing, ever faithful to do only good to them all, to bring blessing out of every seeming bane, joy out of every sorrow, and hope out of despair. We all have our troubles of mind, body, or estate, troubles which press heavily on our beloved, and therefore hurt us most severely ; worse troubles than all, those which are directly traceable to sin in our-selves and others. But there is not one trouble that prayer will not mitigate or remove. "In the multitude of the sorrows that I had in my heart, Thy comforts have refreshed my soul." In the presence of God, we are often taught the good reason why we have been in trouble, often taught how to remedy and escape it, always taught how to bear what is inevitable with patience and hope ; and every one who prays now in earnest shall at last be able to say in triumph : "I sought the Lord, and He heard me ; yea, He hath delivered me out of all my fear."

The foregoing papers on Theism contain the simple beliefs and principles of true religion, the religion of common sense. My next duty will be to defend it against the attacks of a false philosophy and the sneers of a blind and arrogant orthodoxy.

PART VI.

On Anthropomorphism.

An objection has been raised against Theism that it is anthropomorphic ; that, in the language of Matthew Arnold, the God in whom we believe is only " a magnified man "—not a true and real God, but one created by us after our own likeness, one evolved out of our own consciousness.

For readers who may not understand Greek, it may be as well to say that *anthropomorphism*, as used in this connection, means the making of God in the likeness or form of man.

This process has prevailed ever since man began to conceive about a God at all. But the conceptions of God have varied from age to age, and among different races, according to their own development as human beings. The lower the man was in the scale of humanity, the lower and grosser were his conceptions of God. The natural appetites, the fierce, strong passions, the greed, the selfishness, and the cruelty which distinguish the savage, were by him instinctively attributed to his God, so long, and only so long, as he remained unconscious that there was any moral evil in their indulgence. But when the savage began to have moral perceptions, however dim and fragmentary, the fact altered and raised his conception of God. He began to believe in gods and devils too ; in gods who were amicably disposed towards him, and in devils who were hostile and vindictive. His gods he did not think it needful to propitiate or to pray to, while his devils required all his devotion and sacrifice to avert their malice. Then, for a long while, men in this low condition had no distinct consciousness of their own two-fold nature ; they could not imagine themselves to be spirits as well as bodies. The body to them was the whole of a man. Hence their conception of the gods was of beings in a human form, occupying space, localised, measurable, albeit powerful and cunning enough to master and outwit them.

We find even in the Bible traces of this kind of anthropomorphism, where Jehovah is described as toiling and resting, walking in a garden, speaking with audible and human voice, and, later, showing His back to Moses, and His feet appearing as He walked over the firmament ; and, finally, literally dwelling in the Tabernacle and Temple. No wonder, then, that we also find ascribed to Jehovah the weakness and evil passions of man. He is vexed and disappointed at the way in which His own creation had turned out. It repented Him that He had made man upon the earth, and He resolved to destroy the whole human race, save Noah and his family. He is represented as jealous of rival gods, as jealous of His honour, as under the influence of vanity, when Moses prevented Him from an act of fierce vengeance against Israel by reminding Him of what people would scornfully say, and how they would deride Him for not being able to keep His promises to His chosen.

The Jews, we know by their own books, gradually outgrew many of these savage conceptions of their God. One by one the grosser anthropomorphisms were laid aside ; a purely spiritual idea of Jehovah took the place of the animal and material ideas. He had no likeness to anything in heaven above or in the earth beneath ; and little by little the conception of God grew into that of a perfectly righteous God who loveth righteousness, and in whose everlasting arms of love the whole world might lie down in safety.

Alas! contact with polytheistic races prevented the universal adoption of these nobler conceptions of God ; and some Jews, like St. Paul and the writer of the Fourth Gospel, reintroduced the pagan anthropomorphism and the pagan idea of incarnations, and of deified men. The Jews as a nation kept absolutely clear of these corruptions, but the few who founded the Christian Church owed all their success to two distinct but united agencies. The one was the introduction of the loftier morality which characterised Jewish faith and thought; the other was the adoption of pagan anthropomorphism, which enabled the Gentile world to embrace the Christian mythology without any great shock to their own habits of thought.

But it must be owned, also, that the mythology of the Christian faith was far sweeter and more simple than that of the Greeks and Romans, which it superseded; while its anthropomorphic elements were immeasurably less gross, except in one particular. This was the idea that God the Father required, and that God the Son surrendered, his human blood in order to make it possible that God should lay aside His wrath, and that men's sins should be forgiven them. This conception of God was worse than any Greek or Roman myth, and carried the Christian Church back to the worst degradation of the days of Moloch, when men offered their sons and their daughters to avert His displeasure.

Viewing the history of religious ideas in as comprehensive a manner as possible, we cannot fail to see that the rise in conceptions of God has been mainly a process of cutting down and casting away anthropomorphic ideas. We find less and less anthropomorphism as we descend the stream down to our own times. The merely animal attributes have long disappeared from all serious intelligent thought about God. He is not in any one place. He is everywhere, and knows everything, and the very heaven of heavens cannot contain Him; while He is present with all who open their eyes to see Him, and He loves to dwell in the lowly and contrite heart. Not only have the animal human aspects disappeared, but the mental and moral attributes ascribed to God have been vastly elevated. Our conceptions of His mode of producing the cosmos and perpetually changing its outward form have been greatly raised by the discovery of the principles of evolution. Our appreciation of the skill and wisdom everywhere disclosed by the Laws of Nature has led us further and further away from the idea of God as a miracle-monger or a juggler with the forces at His command. And, best of all, our ideas of His goodness and love have led us to abandon the conception of an angry and vindictive God. We cannot any longer ascribe to Him any of our own bad passions or weaknesses. The higher the standard we have set up of *human* excellence, the higher have risen our thoughts concerning Him. And this process is one of the most important ethical facts. Of two men, the one who is more faithful, conscientious, and trustworthy will have a higher conception of God's faithfulness and trustworthiness than the other. Of two men, the one who is most loving, who best knows and practises true fatherly love, will inevitably have a higher and truer conception of the Love of God than the other. It has been by men growing better that their conception of God has risen at all. The process is a matter of present observation, and is beyond dispute.

It is to the increase and development of human sympathy that the doctrine of endless torture in hell is now widely discarded even among Christians, and is destined to disappear altogether. Men cannot believe of their God character and purposes which are below their own standard of common human kindness. Human nature at its highest and best will ever remain—not the measure or limit of what God *is*—but a unit of measure in an infinite round of numbers. It will ever remain as the standard below which God cannot be conceived to be ; the standard by which to test the moral truth of any creed, or so-called revelation, however ancient, however venerable, by whomsoever it may have been first promulgated.

You will now say to me that I have not met the objection, but admitted its truth and its validity. Most certainly I do admit that Theism, like all other forms of belief, is anthropomorphic, and must in the nature of things be so. This is why it is not *final*, but must one day grow into something higher and better. But this is also why it is better than the Christian Faith, why it must supersede that faith. Because, on grounds of fact which cannot be disputed, its conception of God is unspeakably higher and more true than those distinctive conceptions of God which are essentially " Christian."

I repeat that all conceptions of God have been more or less anthropomorphic, and I will now show that it could not be, and cannot be, otherwise.

Every scrap of our knowledge on every conceivable subject is the sole result of human experience. All our thoughts, and, therefore, all our language is limited by experience. We cannot think or speak in terms which are not derived from it. We are, as it were, shut up within a sphere beyond which we cannot pass.

But, nevertheless, within that sphere we find ourselves possessed of reasoning faculties which extend our knowledge far beyond the limits not of our *experience* but of our senses. Among these faculties is the power of imagination, by which we can, so to speak, realise or picture to ourselves much that is unseen. It is, therefore, possible to us to create impossible existences and forms of being which live only in our fancy, and are not in any sense real. But when such creations of the imagination are analysed, we find every separate part of them to be only a reproduction of something which we already know by experience. Such fanciful creations are only grotesque combinations of forms and ideas already suggested by what we have seen and known. There is no other source from which even the most vivid and subtle imagination can produce anything, and I reverently say that God Himself, who has made us what we are and placed us in our present condition, could not make us know or understand anything which transcends our experience, until experience itself is extended to the requisite degree.

It is, therefore, absolutely impossible for us to know the whole truth about God, to understand the mode of His existence, or the exact relation which He bears to the phenomenal world. If any knowledge of Him at all be possible to us, it must be limited to our own human experience. No outside revelation of what is beyond *that* would be intelligible. All the pretended revelations of the world are only the thoughts of men, sometimes wise and true, sometimes foolish and false.

We can, as I have already shown in these papers, know something surely about God, but only by means of what we see and know of ourselves and of the cosmos. We have facts which are simple, intelligible, and indisputable, whereby Reason compels us to infer that a God exists, that He is spirit and not material, that He has certain feelings and dispositions and purposes towards us. But all these thoughts are necessarily anthropomorphic. They are drawn exclusively from what we are, and what we find in ourselves when we try to know what we are. We find that we are spirits, and not merely bodies ; we see the impassable gulf which separates thought from the motion of molecules in the brain ; we feel and know the non-material spiritual emotions of conscience and of love ; and from this common human experience we can pass, without any violation of reason, to the conception of a God who is spirit only, and can be everywhere present, and can know everything. If *we* know a little, a very little, we can grasp the idea of One who knows all things ; still it is anthropomorphic, and cannot be otherwise. The higher side of human nature—the soul or spirit of

———◆———

PART VII

On Moral Evil.

WE come now to consider another objection to Theism, which may be called a philosophical one, but which is certainly not confined to philosophers or pseudo-philosophers. The objection is often loosely designated "Pessimism," which is intended to express the idea that the real evils and so-called evils of the world are incompatible with a belief in a good and loving God, who is at the same time possessed of supreme power. The objection owes all its force to its being based on facts—on the painful facts of human and animal existence. The evils are present and undeniable. How can they be reconciled with the righteous, moral government of the world?

I say, at starting, that hitherto no man has been able satisfactorily to explain *all* the instances of evil which have occurred, or to reconcile every detail with the belief in a good God. But we Theists can rightly claim that we have found satisfactory explanations for a vast amount of pain and sorrow and sin, and that these, when carefully observed, are sufficient not merely to reconcile the evils with a belief in a good God, but largely to increase and strengthen that faith by the disclosure of purposes and methods which reveal a far higher wisdom and goodness in God than were heretofore imagined. In our view, the grounds on which the pessimistic objection is urged become the grounds for a still stronger and nobler faith in God. What was brought forward to overthrow that faith is at length seen to establish it more firmly than before. This is our claim, and we ask only for a patient attention to the proofs of its validity.

The "evils" of the world divide themselves naturally into two distinct categories—physical and moral. But by the term "physical" must be understood not only such evils as bodily pain, disease, and death, but also the mental pains of sympathy or sorrow directly arising out of physical evils which fall upon others, not ourselves. The term "moral evil" speaks for itself. It includes every form of conscious guilt, whether of thought, word, or deed—sin against ourselves, sin against each other, and sin against God.

Mankind has so risen in the moral scale that the best of men and women have quite settled the question as to the relative badness of these two classes of evils. They, one and all, are convinced that moral evil is far worse than physical evil. They are always ready to undergo any amount of pain rather than commit sin ; they would deliberately prefer to see their own child lying dead, or the victim of painful disease, rather than to see him convicted of a crime or the victim of some base passion ; and even when men and women have not risen to this standard of moral excellence, all ordinary persons agree that the pains of the world would be comparatively bearable if it were not for the selfishness and wickedness which abound. It is also very generally admitted, even by those who are not religious at all, and very little moral, that many of the physical evils of the world would disappear altogether, or become much more bearable, if the moral evils could be extirpated, if there were no more sins committed, no more vices indulged.

From all this it will be seen that by far the worst evils of the world are the moral evils, and that, therefore, the existence of moral evil in the world is *primâ facie* a ground of accusation against God much stronger than the existence of physical evils. This, then, is my reason for taking up the subject of moral evil before that of physical evil.

As before, we argue only from facts. We deny or ignore no fact, however apparently hostile to our theory. If we prove our point, it will be on the ground of fact alone.

Now, let us enquire : What really constitutes

"moral evil"? Not certain actions, but conditions under which certain actions are done. We attribute no moral evil, say, to the tiger for killing and eating a man, because, rightly or wrongly, we assume that the tiger is destitute of the moral sense. In killing and eating a man the tiger does not know that its action is right or wrong. The action has no moral quality at all. The same may be said of the human being who is a congenital idiot, or who has become mad and commits a murder while deranged. Not only judges and juries, but all sensible men and women, do not impute moral evil to any criminal who has perpetrated crime while really insane. The action in that case is neither moral nor immoral, but it is *un*moral, like the act of the tiger. Moreover, apart from insanity, we never think of ascribing moral evil to savages, who do actions which *we* call wicked, while they are wholly unconscious that such actions are wicked. We see and say that they kill and eat their captives in war, either thinking it right to do so, or not thinking it wrong, or never giving a thought as to its morality or immorality at all. Again, some customs—*e.g.*, polygamy and polyandry—are accounted moral in one country, and immoral in another, according to circumstances. What would be considered quite right by one race of people would be considered quite wrong by another. The moral quality of the custom or action is determined by the existence and verdict of the moral sense. If I think that a thing is wrong for me to do, it is moral evil if I do it.

Again I appeal to the human conscience. We never feel guilty, and never can be made to feel guilty, for any disaster which may have happened through our agency, if it did not happen through our negligence or malevolence; if, in short, we could not help it. Some such events will readily occur to you. Neither the action nor the consequences of it can create a sense of guilt (under these conditions), although we may grieve and lament the catastrophe to our dying day. A man may be sorry for the unforeseen and unintended mischief he has done; but he can never feel guilty or repent of it as a sin unless he had the power to prevent it, and knew that he was doing wrong at the time. Have I not now said enough to show that moral evil does not consist in particular actions, but in the conditions under which those actions are done? The conditions are mental and moral. There must be a clear understanding of the act (not necessarily of any of its consequences), and a conviction in the heart or conscience that the action is wrong. Sins of omission—not doing the right thing which we know we ought to do — are exactly similar in principle. Moral evil is not an abstraction, but in every case is a concrete reality, caused by a person doing wrong when he knew it was wrong, or neglecting to do the right thing when he knew he ought to do it.

The next step is obvious. Moral evil is the

result of the possession of a moral sense. It can only be created by that moral sense. Without a conscience there can be no moral evil or sin.

We might have been left like the tiger, and the dire consequences of an almost inconceivable savagery would have flooded the world and bathed all human history in mire and blood; but no one would have been at all conscious that anything was wrong anywhere. A state of absolute unmorality would certainly have produced disastrous effects beyond man's imagination to conceive; but there would have been no moral evil at all. There would have been nothing to reveal to mankind any difference of moral quality between one action and another. All alike would have been steeped in absolute moral darkness, in which right and wrong would have ever remained unperceived and unknown.

That which has created moral evil, then, is the addition to our animal nature of a sense by which we perceive moral differences between certain thoughts, words, and deeds. This moral sense is the gift of God, a most precious and altogether beneficent gift, because it is the only means known to us by which it was possible at all for man to rise above the purely animal condition. Remember, that the "evils" of such a condition would have been unspeakably worse than present evils, and would have been also without a remedy; for no one would have been aware that anything was "wrong," or that it was our duty to exercise self-control, in order to prevent or to mitigate the evils perpetually being inflicted upon each other and ourselves.

The first effect of the moral sense is to create sin, to make us think that we are sinful; and yet this is the first step, and the essential step, towards the attainment of any goodness at all. The entrance of sin into the world was, therefore, no "fall" of man, but a "rise," a real step onwards and upwards towards that goodness which is our destiny. We could never become saints if we had not first been made sinners.

Mere innocence is not goodness. Had we been made, at the first, incapable of moral aberration, we could never have been truly good; only mechanically accurate and well-ordered. People forget that the mere inability to go wrong is of no moral value. The only true morality must be the result of effort, of deliberate choice of good in preference to evil; and, therefore, one must not only have power to discern the one from the other, but be placed in circumstances where both are possible. So God gives us a short tether of real freedom within which it is possible for us to choose to do right or wrong; the choice of right under these circumstances being the only condition under which virtue is possible at all.

No one will need any argument to convince him that the purpose of the moral sense is to make us better than we were before, and ultimately to ensure our moral progress till we have become

perfectly good. The first stage is a good one—
to be ashamed of ourselves—to see and know how
much there is to mend in ourselves and in the
world around us. All the divine action is slow.
Evolution teaches us to discern the quiet patience
of God in developing the intractable elements with
which He has to deal. But it is not wise to complain that we were not made good all at once; for
this, so far as we can see, would be impossible.
Shall we complain that the oak-tree must grow out
of the acorn, or the solar system out of star-mist?
These slow processes seem good in the eyes of that
wise Ruler, and no doubt are not only good, but
the best means for attaining His ends. So if His
purpose be to make all men and women good in
the end, He must *grow* them; He must develop
them. The moral processes are organic, just as the
growth of an oak from an acorn; and if only they
are not to be finally defeated, we may well confess
that His processes are the best that could have
been devised. That they do involve great trouble
and inconvenience to mankind, and are, therefore,
called "evils," I do not deny. What some of us
have yet to learn is that the game *is* worth the
candle, that the cost of attaining moral perfection
is cheap and insignificant, beside the privilege and
the glory of it.

In my next paper I will cite facts which are
easily recognisable and verifiable as to the entrance
and first effects of the moral sense. Meanwhile I
ask my readers to tell me, if they can, of any

explanation or solution of the problem of moral evil which is equal to the one I have advanced, in reasonableness and simplicity ; I ask them to instance any theology or philosophy which accounts so fully for the existence of moral evil, and at the same time reconciles the presence of it with the goodness of that God who rules our world.

PART VIII.

The True " Fall of Man."

THE " Fall of Man" was an early and excusable error into which man stumbled in trying to account for the presence of moral evil in the world. But the error lay not in saying that our first parents " fell " from a state of " innocence," but in saying that they fell from a state of moral perfection— " original righteousness," as it was called. This was a contradiction in terms, because, if our first parents had been morally *perfect*, they would not have fallen before the first temptation, which we are told they did. Moreover, had it been possible, the event would have brought great dishonour upon God. We have no need to go back to legend or to history to understand the true " Fall of Man." What is meant by that expression will be clear to us when we add to it the words " from a state of innocence," and turn our attention to the little children everywhere around us. In them we may behold the actual process of the fall from a state of innocence.

No one will pretend that a new-born babe is

moral being at all. It has no consciousness of any difference between right and wrong. It can deserve neither praise nor blame. It is not moral nor immoral, but simply *unmoral*. We have a proverb expressing the fact: " As innocent as a new-born babe." After a while it becomes conscious of its own existence, though none of us can remember that first awakening to the fact. As soon as it is old enough to receive and understand precepts and prohibitions, its parents or nurses have to give it some kind of command, *e.g.*, " You must not touch that," " You must stay there till I come." Not having the least sense of duty or obligation, the child is pretty sure to break that first command. It may get burned or hurt in consequence, or get slapped or scolded for disobedience. If it obeys, it may get some reward or approbation. And either of these experiences will probably influence its conduct in that particular in future. But, so far, it is only guided in its choice by the pain or pleasure which, it remembers, had followed on obedience or disobedience. It has not yet even begun to be moral. By-and-by the day will come when it has broken a parental command, and instead of merely being afraid of punishment, it will feel deeply ashamed, and sorry for the act itself, feeling for the first time in its life that it ought to obey, and ought not to disobey, its parents. It feels the rightness of obedience and wrongness of disobedience quite apart from their respective consequences. Then the moral sense is born within it, and not before.

Then the child passes from a state of innocence
into a state of guilt, a knowledge that it has lost.
its peace of mind, its self-respect, and is verily
ashamed to meet the loving eyes of father and
mother, ashamed of its sin, even though the sin
could remain for ever concealed from them. The
child has fallen from its state of innocence, but it
has, then and there, by and through its sin, *risen*
from its former wholly animal condition into that of
a moral and spiritual being. In no other way, in
no better way, at all events, could it be raised ; in
no other way could the attainment of goodness be
made possible to it. Remember, that goodness
consists in the love of it, in the preference for
it over evil, in the choice of it instead of evil.
But without knowledge of both, the choice of
goodness would be impossible. Everything is
learnt by contrast. Unless we know what sin is,
we could never hate it. Unless we know what
goodness is, we could not love it. Therefore, we
need to be in a state where we can experience
both, and have sufficient freedom to be able to
choose at all. And out of this " fall " from innocence, this real " rise " into the moral state, the
child may learn, and will learn, how to grow into
moral perfection. It must be a conscious sinner, it
must be ashamed of and sorry for its sin, in order
to become a saint, in order to love goodness.

This is the true story of the " Fall of Man ";
and God is enacting for us the scene every day, if
we will but open our eyes to watch it. And we

see in it God's real method of punishing sin and rewarding virtue. The child first awakened to a sense of sin is far more distressed by its own shame and remorse than it would be by bodily chastisement or by a severe scolding. Scolding has no good effect on the character at all, only on the behaviour, until the sense of shame has been aroused, and then scolding becomes superfluous. If the child, on the next occasion, should do right, the sense of heartfelt satisfaction far outweighs the pleasure of reward, whether by gift or praise. It has the double joy of being at peace with itself and at peace with its lawgiver.

The physical consequences of sin are not always painful, while some consequences of heroic virtue are intensely painful. It is not in these consequences that we must look for God's rewards and punishments, but in the feelings of the heart and conscience, where His eye ever sees, and His judgments never fail to acquit or to convict. If we did but allow common sense to have more control over our thoughts and actions, we should grow up, and be trained up, to hold our conscience in greater regard than we do, and we should regulate our lives and cultivate our character in conformity with the rule that—before all things else—we must do and be that which is right, for goodness' sake, for love of God, and love of men. That rule involves, of course, painful and difficult conflicts with our lower nature, and with base principles which infect our very minds and hearts.

The same sacred awe of Duty, which kept our little fingers from picking and stealing the sugar and the jam, will keep us, when we have grown up, from all unlawful gratification. God makes us more than animals, allows us to become immoral, guilty sinners, in order that we may one day be like Himself in loving and choosing and preferring goodness of our own free will. And do not fear that His purpose will fail. In spite of all our animalism and subtle selfishness, He will cause to grow and flourish and triumph the seeds of goodness which He has sown in all our hearts. We have all taken the first step when we first became conscious of guilt. It will not be the last, but we shall make our road to goodness shorter or longer, smoother or rougher, according to our obedience or disobedience to our consciences. As Tennyson says :—

> Men may rise, on stepping-stones
> Of their dead selves, to higher things.

Conscientiousness is our bliss ; the lack of it is our bane. Of conscientiousness, as of true religion—of which it is an essential part—it may be truly said, " Her ways are ways of pleasantness, and all her paths are peace."

And now I must do a little fighting. An impatient company of listeners are eager to unfold to me the many instances known to them of natural human depravity, manifest even in young children, which, in the opinion of the objectors, proves the taint of the old orthodox " original sin."

It is quite true that children are born with hereditary tendencies to specific vices or virtues. This fact is not sufficiently recognised or remembered by parents. Our habitual sins do transmit to our offspring a tendency to fall into them. Drunkenness and profligacy are well-known instances of transmission by heredity; falsehood and cunning likewise. And, on the other hand, the virtues of parents give their children the advantage of a natural tendency to imitate those virtues, and to make moral conflict all the more easy. So it is very certain that all men do not start from the same moral level; *i.e.*, though all are born innocent, they are not all possessed of equal native tendencies to good or to evil. It is harder for a child of impure parents to be chaste; for a child of liars to be truthful. But I do not see how this can in any way affect God's justice, or hinder His final purpose to make all men good at the last. The law of heredity is a good and just law. It cuts both ways. It immensely increases the responsibility of parents, and deepens their sense of obligation to do right and avoid evil for the sake of their children and posterity; and besides all this, not one of our native faculties is evil in itself. The evil arises from its exercise under improper conditions, and to an improper degree; at a wrong time and in wrong company; from a base motive instead of a good one. All the natural and normal faculties are good in themselves, and are given for a good purpose, and would produce only good if used aright. All our vices are but perversions of innocent or virtuous propensities. In any case, the variation of native tendencies in no way touches my argument as to the origin of moral evil.

I conclude this paper with a few suggestions as to the visible and undisputed results of living in a sinful world like ours.

First, there is the effort made by individuals to conquer the moral evil within them. Without such effort there could be no goodness in us at all.

Secondly, in our contact with moral evil in others, some of the most noble and beautiful virtues are engendered, which otherwise could never have had birth. Sin committed against ourselves begets patience, forbearance, long-suffering, pity, mercy, and forgiveness; we are led by it into the heroic virtue of returning good for evil, blessing for cursing, love for hatred. Man is never so noble as then; and the heart of mankind looks upon such loveliness of character with admiration and envy. Such virtue receives an apotheosis, and the men who show it are called Divine.

But how could any of these beauties of virtue have sprung up at all unless in direct contact and conflict with sin? Shut out moral evil, and you cripple and stunt mankind; you make impossible the higher and highest attainments of moral excellence. In spite of all its awful evils, the world is still a good world, the work of a good God, bearing witness, in many details within reach of our knowledge and experience, to the grandeur and sublimity of its moral purpose, and to the far-reaching love of God, who ordains that men shall rise to real and lofty goodness by personal conflict with moral evil in themselves and in others.

And the lesson to be drawn from the facts when we see them is to use well the little liberty and the little light which God has given in working out our own salvation and the salvation of the world from sin. If we do our part faithfully, we may safely look for His help, and be very sure of our final triumph.

PART IX.

——◆——

On Pain and Sorrow.

By the better part of mankind it is universally
felt that sin is a far greater evil than any bodily
pain, or mental suffering arising out of such pain.
I am sorry to say there are a vast number of us
who feel exactly the opposite, and act as if pain
and earthly misfortune were much worse evils than
sin.

Nevertheless, all men are capable of taking the
higher ground. When they seriously reflect upon
it, most men would rather suffer acute bodily pain
than commit a crime. They would prefer to see
their wives and children cold and stark in death,
rather than see them fall into incurable vice.

So I will take it for granted that the worst evil
which can befall us is to *be* wicked; far worse than
merely being disgraced and locked up in a gaol. I
have already endeavoured to show that sin or
moral evil is consistent with the sovereign rule of
a Righteous God, that it is caused by the light of
the moral sense, added, as it were, to our human

nature, in order to raise us from the purely animal condition in which we are born. I have shown that a fall from innocence is the first step in our endless progress towards real goodness ; and if all this be true, the righteousness of God is abundantly vindicated, even when we are considering the worst of all the evils which afflict mankind. Therefore, it will be a comparatively easier task to prove His righteousness and His love in the appointment or permission of bodily pain and of temporal adversities, not less also of the sorrows caused by sympathy and bereavement.

The only justification for the appointment of pain is to be found in the purpose or purposes for which it is inflicted. I am not so foolish as to think that every single instance of pain and sorrow may be satisfactorily explained. All I can do, and all I shall attempt, is to show that in very many instances pain and sorrow are productive of results highly beneficial to mankind at large, and even to the suffering individuals themselves, which could not be achieved in any other way, so far as we can see. If we cannot vindicate God's goodness and love in every case, and yet can do so in many cases and over wide fields of observation, it is only common sense to give Him credit for a good purpose in those cases also which we cannot explain. And especially is it reasonable to remember the enormous disparity between us and Him as regards our age and His, our experience and His, our wisdom and our skill and His.

First, let us look at the fact that the same organisation which makes pain possible to us is also necessary to give us any pleasure at all. If we could not feel pain, neither could we feel pleasure. Pain is the inevitable consequence of those organs by which we are enabled to have any pleasure at all.

Next, it is an admitted fact that a great deal of pleasure is derived purely from the alternation of pain with it. Where pain is never felt at all, there is no sense of pleasure—*e.g.*, in a healthy state, the action of the heart and lungs does not produce any conscious pleasure. It is only when disease has temporarily deranged these organs and produced pain, that the person so affected derives any conscious pleasure in the action of the heart and lungs when restored to health. There is often pain in desire which creates the pleasure of gratification. Common hunger gives a relish to food like nothing else. And hunger is a kind of pain, becoming more acute the longer it lasts.

Again, it is proverbial that satisfaction of animal wants often produces satiety, or loss of the very pleasure which a moderate or interrupted satisfaction begets. If you think it over for yourselves, you will see how much of your pleasure, both in quantity and quality, is due to alternations with discomfort or pain.

But we must go on to ask, what are the direct uses of pain?

The pains of want or desire are essential to life

itself. If the babe did not pine for its food, it would not feed itself by suction. If its cry of hunger did not pierce the mother's heart, she would not know that the child was hungry, nor, perhaps, care to supply its wants. From these very simple instances you may readily learn that the pain arising from want is necessary to life itself. It is also necessary to warn us from danger. If fire did not burn; or poisons did not injure and destroy; if dust did not make our eyes smart; or smoke did not irritate our bronchial tubes;—we should be quickly injured and destroyed by exposure to those sources of pain. The world is so full of illustrations that it would take a lifetime to recount them. I can only give you a few hints, so that you can find other instances for yourselves. Life is largely preserved through the pains caused by noxious and dangerous objects. The pains are God's warnings and signals of danger.

But, further, pain is the chief cause of the development of our faculties. We say in the old proverb, "Necessity is the mother of inventions." What is that "necessity"? It is the necessity for avoiding pain. Pain is the real mother of inventions. Pain has taught us all we know—is the reason why every art has been invented. It was the agent by which man became a strong and cunning animal, asserting and maintaining his right of supremacy over the animal kingdom. His pain drove him to hunt, drove him to ensnare his prey, drove him to clothe himself, and to build shelters, drove him to lead a domestic and social life, to ward off dangers and injuries by united effort; drove him, in short, to seek in civilisation the greatest possible immunity from suffering, or, at least, the best mitigations of the common lot.

Pain is with us to excite our opposition, to call forth the latent energies which otherwise would have lain dormant and useless. We owe every-thing that we have done, and all that we are, to the battle between humanity and physical pain. It has made us restless and enquiring; all our knowledge has sprung out of pain, just as every man amongst us owes his life to-day to the pangs of hunger which he felt when an infant. Pain has been man's intellectual and physical and moral schoolmaster. Had it not been for pain, and the restless desire to prevent or remove it, there would have been no cultivation of the mind, no discoveries of stored-up treasure, no reading of the wonderful books of Nature which are spread out before us. Our inevitable sufferings have been a perpetual stimulus of our minds to knowledge, of our hands to skill, and, of our social instincts to civilisation. Where are the so-called lower animals in the race of life? Do they not stagnate? Are they not pretty nearly in the same undeveloped, unadvanced condition age after age? Possibly this is owing to the compar-ative ease and happiness of their lot. They do not suffer a hundredth part of the pain that we men suffer. They have very few wants; and remember that every want is a pain in embryo, every unsatisfied desire is painful. These humbler creatures of God have little or nothing to stimulate them to human exertions and human inventions. They are, for the most part, in absolute contentment with their lot, and, though not without occasional suffering, they have no pains like ours to endure. So, merely as animals, we are infinitely benefited and enabled to advance by reason of our far greater and more numerous pains.

It is when we come to man as a moral and spiritual being that we behold the grandest of God's good and loving purposes in the appointment of pain and sorrow. I would fain keep to the last that one quality which all the world recognises as the sweetest, loveliest flower of human nature ; but I cannot restrain myself. I must ask, this moment, Where would sympathy have been in a world in which there was neither pain nor grief? Why, your very word, your golden, heavenly word "sympathy," has no meaning without pain and sorrow. Would you really, deliberately, like to live in a world in which sympathy would be unknown? And yet, as sure as the sunlight never pierces the bottom of a mine, so sympathy would never have shone in a painless, tearless, griefless world. Sympathy! What poet shall ever sing the noble deeds, and the still more noble impulses, engendered by sympathy? She outstrips our best endeavours, our most ardent hopes. No man, no woman even, can keep pace with her angelic speed. We try in vain to maintain even a decent level

with her requirements; our best endeavours to
answer to her claims are but miserable limpings
after all, borne along as we are on the crutches of
human resource. Sympathy is the daughter of
God, brought here by pain to remind us of our
celestial birth, and of the high destiny to which we
shall attain ; and you will be only too ready to say
that the price of human suffering is a cheap one to
pay for such an honour, such a glory, as the power
of sympathy.

Besides this surpassing splendour, there is a
stream of minor virtues engendered wholly and
solely by the conditions of grief and pain. There is
fortitude, the manly power of endurance, which in
itself confers nobility ; there is patience, which
involves acquiescence in a Diviner, more loving, will
than our own ; there is active endeavour to lighten
the burdens of our fellow-men, involving the devotion of a whole life to scientific research for the
sole purpose of reducing or mitigating the sufferings
of the race.

And pain, especially the pang of bereavement,
does bring us home to God. It creates and keeps
alive the sense of dependence on Him, even when
we cannot see why we should suffer. It is good
for us to be afflicted, that we may remember that
we are born for a higher life than this ; that we
may be conscious that there is something for which
we ought to crave, much more precious than mere
animal ease and pleasure.

Pain and sorrow remind us that we are children

of God, and that the virtues which only pain can beget are of infinitely more account to beings such as we than the sufferings of this present life.

And, therefore, pain reminds us not only of God, but of our duty. We cannot look on the suffering and sorrow-stricken world without remembering what a large measure of its pains and woes are our own work, the results of our own stupidity, or criminal neglect, or vicious selfishness and covetousness. It is too often *our* fault when our brethren die of hunger, or we ourselves are smitten by loathsome disease. There is a ghastly list of pains and griefs due to nothing else but sin; and till we have driven every one of these out of the world by faithful obedience to God's laws, we ought, in decency, to be silent of reproach against Him for allowing us to suffer at all.

Let our sympathy have its natural course, and keep us from doing those evil things which produce unnecessary pain. Let conscience be heard to keep us from many a sin, many a folly, which entails disease and suffering on our posterity. Let reason be listened to when she urges us to study God's laws of health and soundness, and to follow them faithfully. And above all, let love have full sway over our hearts and lives, that it may interpret for us all that is yet unexplained in the Divine dealings with us. If we love Him truly, we shall trust Him, and admire the wisdom and goodness of His purposes, even in our greatest afflictions. And if we love our fellow-men, we shall never rest until we have done our utmost to make their burdens light, and to turn their very pains and sorrows into joy.

And let me give you one word of advice, if you happen to be still unconvinced:

Do not be so foolish as to ask *me*, Why does not God effect His good purpose at once without all this distress and bother and pain ?

Ask God this question, who alone can give the answer.

I see that if He wants an oak tree he begins with an acorn, down in the dank, dark earth, its shell rotting away all winter. If He wants a man, He begins with a germ, an infant, and so on.

This is His method—slow growth and progress—much surely being required of His creatures, in co-operation, in the use of faculties already bestowed. We see no sign of haste, no sign of omnipotence,* but proofs everywhere of purpose which is only good and kind. This is enough for me.

---

* By this term I mean that popular idea of omnipotence which ascribes to God the power of doing impossibilities and absurdities.

PART X.

The Life after Death.

If you have followed me so far in my endeavour to justify the ways of God to men, you cannot fail to be impressed by the conviction that, if His purposes be good and kind, if the development of the highest virtue and the enjoyment of the most refined pleasure be the objects aimed at by His discipline of us here on earth, these good purposes cannot be *wholly* achieved unless there be for one and all a life to come, in which the processes may be continued till the end be gained. Clearly the end is not attained in this life; we may almost say, with certainty, it cannot be. Here on earth, we witness only the first beginnings, the first incipient movements of the moral and spiritual life. It is not worth while to argue about that at all. If God's purposes be as I have described them, and if there be no life to come, then He has made of this world a miserable failure, in which there is an enormous amount of useless, purposeless suffering, in which all our highest aspirations are frustrated, and in which we, as moral beings, can find an awful list of impeachments against His goodness. It pertains, therefore, to Theism to furnish the grounds on which we may reasonably hope and expect that for us, and for all mankind, there is a life to come after the death and dissolution of the body.

For my own part, I consider that the remarks with which I have commenced this portion of my essays on Theism are quite sufficient ground for the hope of a future life, inasmuch as it is plain that if the goodness of God cannot be vindicated without it, He would cease to be worthy of our trust and love. Nevertheless, there is so much more to be said in favour of the hope, that it is only right to enlarge upon it. In the first place, we, frail and sinful men and women, with all our faults, have at the bottom of our hearts this one undoubted feeling—we would, if we could, bring every one of mankind to a state of perfect goodness and happiness at last. If we had but the power and the skill to do it, we should not need prompting. We should do it; we should give ourselves no rest till we had done it. Why? Because we have been endowed with some measure of sympathy and love. It is love that would make us do this if we could, and if we knew how. Our loving wish to do it is, in my opinion, a witness for God that He certainly will do it, because He can, and because He knows how. We cannot be more loving than God. Surely our love is in this, at all events, pure and unselfish; it is noble and beautiful, without a trace of meanness or self-interest. For even if you or I could do this for all mankind, except only for ourselves—if we could thus save the world and be ourselves lost—that would not keep us back for one moment from trying to save them. And I venture to affirm that it is not only impious, but silly, to think that our love for mankind is greater than God's love. And the unbending axiom of Theism is that God cannot be below the best and highest of His creatures, nor yet below the best and highest that they can imagine Him to be. Nothing can be too good to be true of God and His purposes.

If, then, words have any meaning, and if God have true love towards us, it is a necessary consequence that He will not part with us; that loving us once, even in our low estate, He will love us for ever, and take more delight in seeing His image ripening in us as the ages roll on.

But, here again, all the force of the argument turns upon what we are, what is our true relation to God, what is there in us to survive. We see that, *in a certain sense*, God cares nothing for our bodies. I do not forget the wonderful and ceaseless bounty which flows from Him on all animal life. But what I am looking at now, as a serious fact, is Death, the universal death which comes and destroys in due time every " body " which lives. The whole scene of animal nature is in a state of flux. No thing " continues in one stay." Accident, disease, or decay makes short work of our bodies. God throws them away, pulls them to pieces, restores them into their original elements or atomic conditions, just as it suits His purpose. I cannot say, then, with any pretence of sincerity or accuracy, that God *loves* any *body*. Now, my parents did love my body—would have grieved sorely had my body been taken from them. A mother weeping over her dying child loves the body of her child, and would never part from it at all if she could help it. I could not, therefore, think of God for one moment as a Father to our bodies. But then our bodies are not *we*; our bodies are only the houses in which *we* dwell, the machinery which *we* use, or the clothing which conceals *us* from each other's eyes.

Our bodies do not partake of spiritual life. They are in no way Divine, or partakers of the nature of God. They are material, physical, and, therefore, mortal and utterly perishable. But *we* do share in spiritual life as thinking beings, moral beings, beings who can and do love. In all this we live, and move, and think, and feel in a region which is *not* material, in a region of thoughts and desires, of emotions and passions, of hopes and fears, not one of which is subject to the laws of matter and motion, but lies wholly in another and a higher sphere.

And it is here alone that we recognise what we really are, and what is our relation to God, and what there is in us that can survive. Herein we discover our Divine parentage, our real sonship to

God, our affinity with supreme intelligence, righteousness, and love. Herein we see that God is our
real Father, that we are " begotten, not made," and
that He can love what will never die; that His
Fatherly love is not to be looked for among the
material things of earth, among the bodies of
animals, or the petals of a rose, but in the world of
souls, which are dearer to Him than a babe to its
tender mother. What God loves, in that true and
higher sense, far higher than mere provision for
bodily wants, He will not part with, He cannot lose.
Deny the existence of the soul; deny the love of
God towards it, if there be a soul, and not a trace
of ground is left on which to build any hope of
immortality for man. And then, in the waste
howling wilderness which you have created by
your denials, you have made God Himself guilty
of " a blunder infinite and inexcusable."

And I would wish you to observe how perfectly
futile it is to think to overthrow the hope of a life to
come by asking questions as to how such a life can
be made possible after the death and dissolution of
the body. This is one of the things kept purposely
from our knowledge by God Himself, who knows
to what bad purposes such knowledge might be
put, and how His purpose might be defeated or
hindered thereby. Or, supposing Him to be willing
that we should know all about it, in all probability
no words could possibly describe it to us, for it
takes experience to enable us to understand
anything. Even God could not impart to us

G

knowledge unless we first had the faculty of receiving it. Besides that, men are quite discontented enough with their earthly lot; they might be still more discontented with an insight into the next. The best preparation for another life is to have made the best of this one.

Not pretending to *know* details, we may yet well believe, arguing from analogy, that our life to come will be progress, slow or rapid according to our own use of it; that there will be no jumps or leaps into unearned joys, or translations into a heaven for which we are not fit. We shall have to work out our own salvation *there* as well as here, and it will depend on our own willingness and earnestness to work together with God, whether we attain sooner or later the end for which we were born, and for which our bodies die.

Theism does not concern itself with any of the details and methods of what that life to come may be. Its one trust is in the true Fatherly love of God, which is sure to devise and to carry out all that is best for our welfare.

Some may wish to ask me, as I have been asked many a time, What about the wicked? What will be their future life? And I have found such curiosity suddenly and remarkably chilled by asking them in return: The wicked? How do you know that you are not one of "the wicked" yourself? Have you ever duly considered what ideal justice would say? Is not "wickedness" to be measured in every case by ability or inability to have done better? Advantages and disadvantages differ so enormously that men do not all alike start at the same moral level; and if I, with my unspeakable advantages, have failed in doing what I could do, and what I know I ought to have done, then I am one of "the wicked," and God only knows how much worse I am than "this publican," or "this harlot," whom, in my stupid and blind self-righteousness, I may have despised!

Depend upon it, God will be a fairer Judge than any of us, and we shall get, each and all, exactly the right discipline we may need for the cleansing of our sinful hearts from the love of sin.

When we are once assured of a life to come, on the reasonable ground of God's purposes of goodness and love towards us, we see many other reasons why it would be right for us to live on after death.

The aspirations of man, which he did not create, but which God Himself has implanted, need to be satisfied, if we are to take into account the righteousness and justice of God. Our proper craving for a wider and deeper knowledge of the wonders of the world; our longing for enlarged capacities of useful service; and our thirst for truth in every department of thought—all point to a time and condition in which it would be only right to gratify such lofty hopes. Far more important are those secret longings of the soul for goodness, for a complete weaning from the love of sin, and a heart wholly set upon righteousness.

How we long and pray to *be* good, not merely
to abstain from wrong actions and to do right
actions, but to have clean hearts and right
spirits, and to do always the best with the purest
motives, and to be entirely what the Righteous
Father wishes us to be! Not to satisfy such
longing as this would hardly seem right in the
eyes of a true moral judgment. Then, again,
there is our pure and unselfish love, so bitterly
wounded by bereavement. Would it not be in
the highest degree right and just to allow to that
old love its full fruition in a life where separation
would be impossible? or, if for wise purposes
separation were allowed, it would always be
certainly followed by reunion. And is the
discipline of this life so perfectly clear to one
and all that there is no need for explanation, no
need for a higher standpoint to enable us to see
the goodness and wisdom, which, here below,
we cannot always discern? Much as Theism
has already said to reconcile us to God's dealings,
it cannot solve every problem, or cast light strong
enough to make visible every detail of the Divine
dealings. We do want a wider range and improved
faculties for such a stupendous research.

And I, for one, reverently declare my conviction
that it would be only right in God to clear up
for me, some day, every present difficulty, and
to remove every cloud which our earth-born mists
have cast up between ourselves and the brightness
of His face.

But all these are minor arguments compared with the one supreme ground of our hopes :—

God loves us all, just as we are, with an ever-lasting love, and that means that we can never perish nor remain in endless sin and misery.

"Now Lord, what is my hope? Truly my hope is even in Thee."

"As for me, I will behold Thy face in righteousness, and when I awake up after Thy likeness I shall be satisfied therewith."

PART XI.

The Moral Value of Theism.

WE have now gone over the principal beliefs of Theism, and the grounds of fact and reason on which it rests. It remains now to show how, in addition to the unspeakable comfort and hope which it affords, it is the greatest possible aid to morality. For it will be admitted, on all hands, that religion is a sham and a farce unless it helps us to be more faithful in duty, to grow better from day to day, or, at least, to keep us from degenerating into a lower moral condition.

And the principle of Theism is, that as it sets before us God in the most lovable aspect, as it teaches the entire friendliness and matchless love of God towards us, it thereby invokes and inspires our love to Him in return, the love of gratitude and the love of admiration. And in so far as this love toward God is sincere and strong, it must produce in us a most fervent desire to do His will, *i.e.*, to do what is right, and to forsake what is wrong. Further still, it impels us to desire to *be* right at heart, to be good in secret where no eye but God's can see, to be set free from the love of sin, which is the one foe we have to fight from the cradle to the grave.

And inasmuch as we can render no service to God except in and through the service we can render to our fellow-men, it follows that he who most desires to please God will be the most loving, and faithful, and true, and trustworthy towards those among whom he may be placed. It is well known that the most conscientious man is always the best trusted by his fellows, whether they be good or not. It is well known that the most loving man is always the best loved. Therefore, conscientiousness and love require no further re-commendation. The verdict of humanity is passed that these are the best gifts which any man can possess.

The Theist maintains that these faculties are immensely strengthened and enlarged by Religion, by remembering God, by a sense of duty towards Him, by deep gratitude for His goodness, and by love and admiration of God Himself. The Theist pleads for the acceptance of his thoughts about God and His dealings on the ground that they offer no stumbling-blocks in the way of our perfect trust in Him. Theistic thoughts of God are free from countless blemishes and inconsistencies, which either puzzle the mind of the seeker after God, or openly blacken His face and tarnish the lustre of His moral perfections. We know but little, it is true, of all that may yet be known of God and His goodness ; but even that little is enough to make all men declare—and feel, if they will not declare— that it is the best and highest and most attractive of all the conceptions of God hitherto proclaimed.

All that is wanted is that men should believe it, and feel it, and act upon it, and henceforth discipline their own lives and character in accordance with it.

There is, first, the thoroughness of it ; the tackling with evil at its root, the cleansing of the heart and the motives, the enlisting of our affections, as well as our conformity, on the side of obedience. Then there is the hope of success, the absolute certainty of growth towards the attainment of our noblest aspirations. God will not leave us in the lurch, if we will only hold by His hand and look up to Him for guidance and strength. It is true, and grandly true, that He will never compel our obedience, and can never *drive* us to love Him. But He can and will, if we let Him, draw our hearts towards Him and kindle our love to Him by the sight of His love to us. He promises us the final victory over all evil within and around us ; not in the words of any text, or by voice which may be heard with our outward ears ; but by the experience we have had of what true love is. If we have ever learned that, we have therein His promise to do for us all that true love demands : "O taste and see how gracious the Lord is. Blessed is the man that trusteth in Him."

Then, besides this thoroughness and this hope of final victory, there is the exceeding great and precious joy which is to be found in the honest endeavour to be and to do what God requires. Whatever we do for love is a delight to us. There can be no drudgery in it, nor weariness. The duties which seem so hard, the self-denials which seem so painful, are, by love, transfigured into privileges and enjoyments. Instead of being driven to them, we are drawn; we run gladly to do the work and to endure the hardship for the luxury of gratifying our love to God and men. Life becomes a perfectly new experience. The world is a perfectly new world so soon as love gets hold of us, and we can forget our poor selves in the rapture of true service to others.

Yet another most helpful thought is to be found in our logical conclusion that, because God is the common Father of all mankind, all we are brethren. My heart sinks at the thought, how this grand truth has lost its significance by repetition, how it has become a cant phrase which ends only in sound, and has no practical effect on our lives. But nevertheless it is not quite dead. It will, and must, revive and wield the most potent influence for good over our relations with each other. Especially do we need it in the higher regard for the rights of others than for our own; in thinking more heartily and disinterestedly of our

duties to them than of their duties to us. The
"brotherhood of men" may yet emerge as the
saviour of society when it means just this in every
conceivable relation in life : "Put yourself in his
place. How would you like to be treated as you
are treating him ?" Unless we are deliberate liars
to ourselves, we cannot always face such a question
without guilt and shame. We know, and we ought
to lament it more than we do, that men and women
of every rank and class in life, rich and poor,
employers and employed, have not always felt or
acted towards each other as brothers and sisters.
We want our own hearts set right before we can
reform present abuses and anomalies, or even judge
correctly of the merits of any scheme. In Religion
and not in Secularism lies the poor man's hope.
In brotherly love and not in covetousness will be
found the remedy for all injustice. I, for one, look
to Theism, or to a belief in God higher and better
still when it can be found, to mend all the evil
ways of the world, to abolish envy and covetousness
from all hearts alike, to abolish criminal self-seek-
ing and selfish neglect of our brethren, to drive
away all strife, bigotry, persecution, and to trample
in the mire our base, our contemptible, ambitions.

It will yet break the neck of tyranny, whether of
potentates, parliaments, or mobs ; it will destroy
the noxious elements alike in wealth and in
poverty ; it will breed universal contentment only
by kindling universal love. For the more we love
God, the better shall we love one another. In

striking contrast to a religion which teaches " Whoso loveth father or mother, son or daughter, more than me, is not worthy of me, and cannot be my disciple," Theism teaches that we cannot love each other too much, so long as it is true and not sham love ; and that the way to please our Father best is to love each other with a pure heart fervently.

And one word more on this theme, which, if we do not remember and act upon, all our work and time and thought will be thrown away: We cannot be true Theists at all unless we become so by giving our hearts to God, and trying to do His will, and to love and serve each other. We literally cannot know God as our Friend and loving Father unless we know a little of the blessedness of human friendliness and human love. This is the door by which alone we can enter into the unspeakable privilege and joy of knowing God at all. To the utterly selfish heart there is no possibility of knowing or loving God.

So, if we pray, as all men ought to pray, to be able to know, love, and serve God, we must add to our prayers every thought, word, and deed of kindness, sympathy, and brotherly love which we can think, speak, and do. Thus, and thus only, can we work out our own salvation from sin, and taste and see how gracious the Lord is.

PART XII.

Theism contrasted with Christianity.

In this, my twelfth and last of the papers on Theism, which the editor of *The Weekly Times and Echo* has so generously allowed me to contribute, it will be my duty to say some painful words, perhaps all the more to be listened to and weighed on that account, seeing that I am a human being and would not willingly wound other people's feelings. I shall have to show how far, if Theism be true, it comes into collision with the orthodox Christian beliefs.

Persons who do not see very far beyond the immediate present have often said to me, " Why do you not leave other people's beliefs alone ? Why are you not content with simply stating that which you believe to be true, and let it work its own way quietly without raising controversy ? " This plausible plea, often suggested by good motives, might have some weight if the facts of history did not betray the fallacy. Without controversy, no change, no progress, no real improvement would have been possible. Christianity itself, a vast improvement on the Paganism which it supplanted, owed its conquests and its triumphs entirely to the controversies carried on by its founders. St. Paul could do nothing without it. His Epistles teem with it ; and all who had anything to do with the promulgation of the Gospel had to fight with existing errors and superstitions as well as to proclaim the purer and nobler truths.

Now, if you have to teach arithmetic to children or others who have never had any arithmetical instruction before, your obvious duty would be to confine yourself as a teacher to the positive truths of arithmetic—*e.g.*, the multiplication table, as we know it—and it would be folly for the teacher to drag in specimens of false arithmetic in order to prove the superiority of the true. But supposing his pupils had all been trained up in a false arithmetic, and had learned a false multiplication table—as, for instance, " Twice two are five, and three times one are one "—then it would be absolutely necessary for the teacher not only to teach the true multiplication table, but also to point out wherein the false one was false, and to draw the contrast again and again until the pupils had entirely unlearnt the false one.

Now this is exactly parallel to the relations of Theism and Christianity (I will say *orthodox* Christianity, lest some heretical Christians be disturbed by the unqualified term). The teacher of Theism, deeply convinced that it is true, or at least far more true than any other faith, and desirous above all things to teach people to believe it, finds himself confronted with a mass of his countrymen who have been taught to believe much which is wholly opposed to Theism, and which is, therefore, by hypothesis, wholly untrue. These false beliefs are so deeply ingrained in every fibre of their minds and hearts, that it is extremely difficult to dislodge them. The case in Theology is far worse than in that of a false arithmetic. To believe that twice two are five, or three times one are one, though extremely inconvenient to the mis-taught person, certainly can make no difference to his eternal welfare, nor would arouse the anger of God; whereas the belief in Christian dogmas is a matter of even more than life and death—is a matter of endless joy or endless torment ; so that any one believing those dogmas runs an awful risk (so he has been taught) in denying or doubting them for a moment. Even putting aside the awful eternal consequences, believers in Christianity have been taught that at least God will be dreadfully angry with them if they do not believe the whole Bible, or the atonement by Christ, or if they question for one instant the teaching and the authority of " the Church." All this makes the work of the Theist so much harder, and the duty of controversy so much more imperative, because if Theism be true and orthodoxy false, men's minds must be first brought round to see that it is no sin to read, and enquire, and to think for themselves ; that the dear God in heaven will not be angry with them for using the sacred faculties which He has given for the very purpose of seeking and finding Him, but that it will please and delight Him to behold His children *bent fearlessly on searching into the truth of things*, and weighing, one against the other, the discordant cries of human teachers. Theism thus comes into conflict with Christianity at the very outset, and claims, in the name of the Righteous, Loving God, men's right to think for themselves, and urges the paramount duty of doing so. (N.B.—That Church condemns itself which teaches that it is a sin, a heinous sin, to use our own God-given faculties in criticising Church dogmas or the Bible.)

I will not attempt to illustrate all the points of contrast between Theism and orthodox Christianity. I will take only the distinctive idea or belief which runs through every form of it, from the Church of Rome down to the smallest and obscurest of Christian sects. I state it in the baldest, barest terms, not to hurt sensitive minds, but only to avoid mistakes. All Christians, except those who call themselves " Unitarian Christians," believe :—

That one God sent another God from heaven to earth, to live, suffer, and die in a human body, in order to save mankind, or some portion thereof, from a frightful doom, described in the New Testament as a "curse." This universal belief, enshrined largely in Creeds and Liturgies and Sacraments, Articles of Religion, Councils of

Trent, Confessions of Faith, and Catechisms, involves and implies that the death of Christ and the shedding of his blood was so necessary for our salvation that, without it, God could not, or would not, be a loving Father and Friend to man, but would sentence them, or leave them to fall helplessly, into everlasting torment and sin.

To save us, or some of us, from this curse, was the sole reason for the Incarnation of the Son of of God on earth, for his sufferings, and for his death.

If this be true, then these conclusions certainly follow :—

1. There are two Gods. One who became incarnate, and the other who never was incarnate.

2. There are two Gods, one of whom is represented as saving us by his own sufferings from the awful wrath and vengeance of the other God.

3. There are two Gods, one of whom men cannot help loving supremely, while they hate or dread the other.

4. One of the two Gods is represented as unjust beyond all human injustice, sentencing to everlasting perdition the whole race of mankind for the sin of their first parents ; as cruel, beyond all human cruelty, in keeping alive for ever, in torment and in sin, creatures who were, without their consent, born into the world frail and weak and easily tempted. This God is represented as demanding the sacrifice of human blood to appease His wrath and to cancel His sentence of doom. For a thousand years it was

commonly taught that the shedding of Christ's blood was the price paid for our ransom to the Devil, till Anselm arose and showed that this idea was wrong and contrary to the New Testament, and that the blood of Christ was the price paid for our ransom to God the Father. This has been taught in Christendom ever since.

5. The fifth conclusion is obvious, and is verified at this day, viz. : That Jesus Christ has taken the place of the living God, our Father, in the affections of men. That the Father, to whom even Jesus himself prayed, and to whom he taught his disciples to pray, is either an object of dread, or is altogether overlooked and disregarded, while Jesus is worshipped, trusted, and loved in His place.

"Out of Christ," as the phrase is, God is an unspeakable horror, the fierce and relentless foe of mankind ; but "in Christ" God is all love and compassion. The whole system of mediation turns upon these Christian thoughts about God. The whole Sacramental system and the arrogant claims of the Church likewise depend on the primary and fundamental belief that there was an awful doom decreed by one God against us, and from which we can only be delivered by the sacrifice of the other God.

Now, as a teacher of Theism, and indeed more still as an earnest seeker after God and His truth, I am bound to place in open contrast this Christian idea of God's wrath and the scheme of salvation with the simple and sublime idea of God as a loving

Father. Not I alone, but we are all bound to ask and go on asking, " Which of these ideas of God is true, and which is false ?" Both cannot be true, though both may be false. The contradiction is so complete that they cannot be harmonised. The Christian does not really worship and love the same God as the Theist does. The God of the Theist is the Eternal, Righteous Father of all men, who is ever so near and close to His children that an incarnation like that of Jesus Christ would be not only superfluous, but would create a gulf between God and men which never existed. And if God be our Father in deed and in truth, mediation and intercession would only distress and insult Him.

Then, again, our Father punishes us for sin, only to correct and amend us. If so, we cannot afford to lose a grain of His chastisement; and, therefore, an atonement, a sacrifice, or propitiation, which would save and screen us from God's punishments, would be no blessing at all, but a curse—not a deliverance, but a doom.

Again, unfortunately for those who worship Christ as God, and love him supremely, his alleged history is reported in the four Gospels, wherein he is made to say and do things which only reflect discredit on him as a man, which betray errors of a very serious kind, concerning both God and man, some of his sayings being deeply at variance with other sayings of his which were lovely and true, so that we have not even the picture of a perfect man before us, much less of a perfect God.

Now I say that it corrupts the heart as well as confuses the mind to worship and love supremely, as a God, a human being with at least some of the frailties and errors which belong to us all. It is dishonouring to God to put any creature in His place. " The deification of Jesus is the grand historical testimony to the meanness of man's thoughts about God." It is, then, I plead, a matter of supreme and solemn importance to us all, not to rest satisfied till we have found out which is true and which is false—Theism or Christianity. It concerns not only us private individuals, but every Bishop, every dignitary, and every clergyman of the Church of England, and all the ministers of every other Church or sect in Christendom. To point to the Bible, or to the Church, and say that either or both of them have already closed the question, is to impute folly or wickedness to the Most High—as though, in such a solemn theme as this, God had first given us faculties for the discovery of religious truth, and then instantly had forbidden us to use them ; and as though, in such a transcendent matter as the Incarnation of a God to save the world from everlasting sin and torture, He has given not one single proof that the New Testament contains no errors, has not given us any evidence whereby we can positively be assured which out of all the claimants is the true and infallible Church. The New Testament is full of contradictions. It even casts discredit upon the Incarnate God whom it professes to depict ; and " the Church " is an angry mob of conflicting rivals, each one reviling the other for what they call " damnable heresy."

The hope of unity amongst the Christian Churches and Sects is further off than ever. Men will only unite by common assent to that which makes the strongest appeal to their best thoughts and feelings.

If they will be but in earnest ; if they will but surrender themselves to the dear Father in heaven, and beseech Him to teach and to guide them ; if they will but use the faculties within them, their reason, their conscience, and their natural human love ;—these will teach them all that is best and truest the world has ever known or heard of; and this assuredly will bring them into far closer harmony of belief than any Church has done before. It will not make them infallible, it will never permit them to make so silly, so mischievous, a pretence ; but it will enlighten their minds, quicken their consciences, and kindle the flame of sacred love both to God and men. Religion is a grand help to us in the faithful discharge of the duties of this life, and of the service we owe to each other. But religion is of greater value to us the more true and simple and pure our creed is, and the more closely it binds us in love to our God. So for man's sake, as well for the sake of truth and God, I beseech you, look into this great matter without delay, and may God enable us all to come to a right judgment !

www.ingramcontent.com/pod-product-compliance
Lightning Source LLC
Chambersburg PA
CBHW032145010726
47493CB00008BA/2586